GOD OF THE PIGEONS

JAY MERILL lives in central London and is a freelance editor and co-organiser of the spoken word event, Ride the Word. Jay received an Arts Council England award for an individual artist, which enabled her to have increased time to write this, her second short story collection, in which she pursues themes of illusion, fantasy and a desire for transcendence. Jay walks a lot in urban spaces. What she passes through fleetingly enters the world of her stories. Movement and pace are essential ingredients in Jay's work. Her first short story collection, *Astral Bodies*, was nominated for the Frank O'Connor Award, and was a clear short story winner in the Salt 'Just One Book' readers' vote on the most important book ever published by Salt.

Jay Merill
God *of the* Pigeons

CAMBRIDGE

PUBLISHED BY SALT PUBLISHING
14a High Street, Fulbourn, Cambridge CB21 5DH United Kingdom

All rights reserved

© Jay Merill, 2010

The right of Jay Merill to be identified as the
author of this work has been asserted by her in accordance
with Section 77 of the Copyright, Designs and Patents Act 1988.

This book is in copyright. Subject to statutory exception
and to provisions of relevant collective licensing agreements,
no reproduction of any part may take place without the written
permission of Salt Publishing.

First published 2010

Printed in Great Britain by the MPG Books Group, Bodmin and King's Lynn

Typeset in Swift 11 / 14

*This book is sold subject to the conditions that it shall not,
by way of trade or otherwise, be lent, re-sold, hired out,
or otherwise circulated without the publisher's prior consent
in any form of binding or cover other than that in which
it is published and without a similar condition including this
condition being imposed on the subsequent purchaser.*

ISBN 978 1 84471 772 9 paperback

For Avrina

CONTENTS

God of the Pigeons	1
Medusa	9
Squeeze	18
Mimosa, House of Dream	23
Little Elva	31
The Deus ex Machina Bird	36
Can I be Dandini?	49
Beauty Queens	56
Making Dracula	68
Racetrack	76
Batman	82
See You Later, François Marie	89
Entertaining Angie	100
My Secret Rollerskates	105
Clouding the Light	113
Riddle	122

GOD OF THE PIGEONS

Azi and Rob have just moved in to this top floor apartment at the centre of the city. The first thing they notice is the cooing of pigeons. Azi says they've moved to Pigeon Land. The apartment block is large and looming, there's a weightiness of dark red brick. In the bedroom they uncover a dramatic fireplace, cast iron with a bell-like dome, ceramic tiles with the glaze unveined running down each side. Embossed twined flowers, early 20th Century art nouveau. The aperture to the chimney is blocked off with a piece of wood but that's alright, the room's too small for an open fire. Azi stands a house plant in the grate. Leaves and tendrils. What a focus it gives the room this fireplace with its embellishments. *Like an altar*, she thinks. They paint the room a pale goldyellow.

This bedroom is at the side of the building towards the rear, and the window faces out over a gully on the other side of which is another apartment with a window in the same position. Azi thinks how beyond the window there's probably a bedroom just like theirs with an identical fireplace, and on the other side of that apartment another gully, and then another apartment and so on for the whole length of the road. It's strange to her, lying in bed and thinking of this endless line of other bedrooms. The rear of each apartment is a grey precipice and Azi has a sense of the interiors as remote islands of habitation which the buzz of the surrounding streets can hardly penetrate. The city is made up of such islands.

The gullies between the apartments are narrow and dank, nobody ever goes there. Azi and Rob lie in bed winter afternoons. They live on the top floor and can see the chimney on the roof of the apartment

GOD OF THE PIGEONS

opposite, dense against clear sky; they can see the window of a kitchen. Frosted glass which you can't look into. Cut into the glass is an extractor fan which spins round and round whenever the people who live there pull the cord. Azi and Rob do not know these people, have never even seen them. To Azi they're an interesting mystery, dim shadowed forms behind the glass; the pulling of the cord, the whirring of the fan, strange ritualistic events. She has a love of this mysterious city where things can be happening right next to you yet are still unknown by you. *Living in a city is like being on a far off island*, Azi thinks. Thousands of islands all cut off by gullies, yet all belonging to one another.

In summer they lie in bed in the heat, close up to the open window, watching the whirring movement of the fan and hearing the cooing of pigeons on a window ledge, or the plock plock of tennis balls onto the courts at the back of the apartment block. Lying here right next to the city sky, Azi says she feels they're in communion with the God of the Pigeons. All strangely quiet. Just the birds, this faint whirring of the electric fan in the window across the gully and the plocking sound. Here and there a voice will drift up. A murmur or an echo. Sometimes they see the mauvepurple shapes of pigeons taking flight.

A morning comes, just into winter. There's a tinge of sharpness reminding them of frost. Azi and Rob hear a scuffling and scratching in the chimney which keeps on getting louder then subsiding.

'D'you think a bird is trapped inside?' Azi asks unwillingly.

In one of the quiet patches between the scufflings they both say, 'No, it can't be a bird.' When the scratching gets intense they say, 'If it's a bird it'll get out.'

Then comes the weekend, they're going away. Which is how it happens they don't know when the scraping stops and silence begins. They'd wished for the noise to end and it's ended in their absence. But sometimes it works out better to be present at the finality as then there's a point to recover from.

They've come back. Winter is more entrenched, the air is chilled, frostier, there's no more scuffling in the chimney. They go to bed that first night happy and relaxed, not even remembering there had been scuffling, just being easy because it's not going on. In the morning they sit up in bed with coffee mugs balanced on their knees.

'What's that?' Azi, her voice wavery and quiet because of the unwillingness to see what she's seeing. 'Rob, what *is* that?'

The wing of a pigeon hangs in a sleek feathered triangle, in a V of white and grey; it hangs stiffly, pointing down towards the grate. In the chimney a dead bird is concealed, the wing protruding through the narrow slice of space to one side of the boarded-up aperture. Now it's no longer possible to think of the room as simply next to the sky. It's gained in complexity, the chimney-space is an intervention they will have to reconcile themselves to. In this space a pigeon has fluttered, has scraped its body against rough chimney walls, unable to get out. They try not to picture the bird as it had been, or its fall, or the inside of the chimney, sooty at the base, with this same bird, dead, resting against the wood on the side where it hasn't been painted white. But Azi lets out a sharp painful cry, because in trying *not* to picture things you can be etching them in very distinctly.

'There was a bird trapped inside, I told you, but you said it wasn't there,' they both say. 'You said it could get out. Now look! Look what's happened. It's unbearable.' Then a violent rattling of coffee mugs, a morass of spilt coffee as knee humps spoil. A scream, a hollow shout, a real desire to get far away from here. Of course they see they'll have to unblock the chimney and remove the body of this bird.

On the day after they've cleared the soot from the chimney and swept it, along with the heavy body of the dead bird, into a plastic bag, there's a feeling of peace. The bad things have been removed, the bag disposed of, the wood replaced. There's a back to normal ease about them, a done and dusted composure. How great not to have the intrusion of scuffling, how especially great to have got rid of the vicious triangle of wing. Uncanny and horrible how it had found the small slit at the bottom of the wood and come through like that.

GOD OF THE PIGEONS

But it's not that easy to forget. Rob knows the pigeon is dead, its pain over, but he's unhappy, sits all quiet with his perched coffee mug and doesn't drink, or speak to Azi. He's thinking of the irrevocability of things. The bird's suffering has happened—a truth which can't be wiped away by anything else. There can be no alleviation for that past suffering. He even regrets that the horror *is* over, because it's being over that seals it. Anger and even fear sneak up on him. He'd like to change things, but how can you change what's already happened? He can't drink the coffee today, it tastes too weird, tastes of impossible lateness, of closing the door when the horse has gone; has a metallic tinge to it that may be the kettle, it may be the water pipes, but to Rob it tastes of failure. There's blue sky showing through the window, enticing, wintry. But how can he enjoy the sight of sky in which the pigeon has once flown? And he's bothered by the tunnel of space within the chimney. An invisible room.

Azi's sad because of the silence and the bird. Their bedroom itself seems like a torture chamber, the walls wicked and hollow, such a poisoning of their lovely space. How unendurable for this to happen in a love nest, a room where only happiness was to flow. The V of the birdwing is the worst of it. There's a lasting impression of that in Azi's mind, hard to resist seeing it as an omen, some sinister reflection of her life and the way it's going. She's got this bad feeling that once a sight such as this reaches you it'll be locked forever in your memory bank, it will never be nowhere. The unforgettable V, and the unstoppable pull in Azi to make negative meanings out of it. At the same time she's experiencing this deep charge, seeing winter sun through the filmy curtain. Vivid lemon. Sees with almost too much detail, the weave of the curtain, a web of hairline cracks on the walls, a small coffee stain the shape of a bird's head. But she's also having bad feelings about the structure of the whole building. Nothing seems solid. She pictures gaps and hollows, hidden spaces behind the walls.

Rob's trying not to indulge in self-reproach, because, how will this help? It won't. Even so, the taste of the coffee is bitter, because a mental state needs its own outlet, regardless. It's not that in the back of his mind he's saying, *Why didn't I?*, or *I should have*, or *What if I'd . . . ?*, but even so. He sits up in bed mentally reconstructing the chimney space, not looking at the sky, feeling that he himself is an irrevocable fact set down once and for all just as he is, with a bird's capacity for falling. He mourns his lack of freedom. For Rob *fixed* equals *finished* and he feels a multitude of angers all to do with not giving in. To images, to the past, to what's set down as history. He sits hollow as a chimney, this battle raging desperately inside him, his wings colliding with walls; carrying on fighting a war which is already lost—because it has to be.

Rob thinking: It's hard to imagine the pigeon could have died in that chimney, now it's all over, hard to believe there was a slit at the bottom of the wooden panel of a sufficient width for the insertion of a pigeon wing. He laughs silently at the crazy improbably of the bird wing so positioning itself as to find this slit and neatly drop itself down into the fireplace. But it *did* happen.

Azi sipping at her cooling coffee, looking up at sky. The coffee and the sky are making her shudder. She notices the window opposite, across the gully, thinks, It's strange there are people living there I've never seen. Sometimes I notice their shadows through glass or hear water gushing into drains on hot afternoons. Winter and summer the extractor fan whirrs round and round whenever somebody pulls the cord. Other than that, these people, it's hard to believe they exist. She thinks of pigeons in the city. Pigeons outside your window of an early winter morning billing and cooing and perching on chimney pots, sometimes falling.

Rob and Azi lying together not quite in harmony, not quite out of it. Bed by the window, a desert of cream cotton. Thinking inevitably about the bird; they can't seem to let go. There's a feeling in both of them that their life here in this room, in the apartment, is spoilt, a taste of poison about everything now. It's starting to be clear they might have to move out, a bit drastic, but they can't seem to stop their emotions being dominated by thoughts of the pigeon. Yes, they're both beginning to see that at some point they'll have to get out of here. Bad associations, you can't fight them. And even then they might never enjoy the taste of coffee again. They won't know why it is, they'll have forgotten, edited out the details, but they'll make a face when they see other people drinking the stuff, because it's probably true that what you've forgotten is at least as powerful as what you remember.

They feel different about the city now, and this island room they used to love so in those first days. They feel restless and confined, as though they're prisoners in very little space. Azi doesn't like looking at the sky because of the protruding sight of the rooftop. She says there's a hemmed in look, a sky should be large and wide. A city sky has a sad something about it. She's gone off the idea of living in the city altogether. It makes her feel ill, and she doesn't mean the pollution, it's the isolation she's talking about. *I mean what sort of a world is it where you don't know your neighbours?* is what she now says.

The gully is a deep moat surrounding a fortress. The plocking of tennis balls is no longer comforting, it's an abrasive staccato, could be the sound of machine-gun fire. One of the saddest things about the way they are is their pessimism — they seem to be in competition for seeing the worst in everything. Only bad interpretations satisfy them they're not living an illusion. And either one of them sometimes has a dream in which they're trapped in a vertical tunnel at the top of which the sky can be seen but never reached. They flap and whirr and scratch till an invisible hand leans down and pulls a cord. Then they'll wake up and say *I had that dream again*, there's a grim satisfaction in it. So, the catastrophes of pigeons and humans, who both fall blindly in their distinctive ways.

Winter and spring pass, it's summer now. One hot Sunday afternoon with the window open. Azi and Rob are lying on the bed. Slow drift of the long nearly see-through curtain. Wind from the gully ruffles its floating edge, sunshine sprays the gauzy fabric. All's quiet except for the balls on the tennis courts with their plock, plocking. The plastic ventilator in the frosted-glass window the other side of the gully begins to whirr. It's peaceful here, but it feels like the wrong kind of peace.

GOD OF THE PIGEONS

They're both irritated by the murmured disturbances of summer. Azi has come to the point of saying she'll scream if she has to hear the plock of one more tennis ball.

And things aren't so good between the two of them. They used to lie in one another's arms, stroking, smoothing skin, licking, kissing, like two cats. Now they keep to opposite sides of the bed hardly ever touching. There are misunderstandings, they quarrel over little things, and they sigh. These escaped sighs are like hostile statements, flying out and injuring, driving them further into combat. They don't like being together any more so they spend less and less time here—getting out of the apartment is a relief to them. Work, which they used to resent a bit because it kept them apart, is something they now look forward to. Nowadays they never mention the pigeon, what would be the point? They've already said everything that can be said. It's uncertain if they'll stay together now. Summer's turning the city grey and rusty brown.

At last they make the decision to move. The idea begins as pure escapism with no foot in reality, just a pleasure which draws them out, the only good shared feeling. Finally they say to one another, 'Well, why don't we? Get out of the city, start a family.' It's the first time they've thought of a *family*. This starts as a word said, but it too becomes a reality they want. The city isn't the right place for them to be now. All of their needs fit together.

They find somewhere right on the edge of the commuter belt that's amazingly countrified. Rob, for the time being, comes in to town every day to work, but that's not the same. Azi becomes pregnant the same week as moving and leaves work when she's five months. Things pick up for them, their marriage becomes a success story, love has revived. The city is now a remote and hazy place. One of the last conversations they ever have about those early days was just after their daughter Dulsa was born.

The bird dying in the chimney that time—do you remember?—I believe it was a sign to us to get out. A sad thing, wasn't it, but you know praps it was meant to be. I feel it was a symbol of renewal, maybe the universe was trying to tell us something.

I know what you mean, we were moving in a wrong direction, and then the pigeon getting trapped like that in the chimney, terrible thing. As if the chimney was the city and the God of the Pigeons was sending us this warning to get out before it was too late.

The pigeon wing—like a hand pointing clearly to us, saying, 'Go for it.' Spelling out 'Birth' to us. Does that seem silly? To me it couldn't have been more clear.

New people have moved into the apartment. Carla and Steve. 'Such a lovely secluded atmosphere in the bedroom, so quiet,' they say. 'How amazing you can be right in the centre of the city and have such peace.'

They board up the fireplace, although regretting the art nouveau motif, because they're never going to have a fire there anyway. A boarded up fireplace will blend in better with the surrounding walls, will give a smoother overall effect, make the room seem larger. And they can stand the bed there. They paper the room a soft, dreamy blue.

'Listen,' Steve murmurs as they lie in bed late on a Saturday morning with pigeons cooing on the window ledge outside. Carla thinks how even though they've re-done the room it's still the same space that other people have once inhabited. It's strange to her, lying in bed and thinking of an endless line of earlier inhabitants. An archipelago of invisible islands stretching back and back. A city is made up of such islands. 'I feel as if we're linked to the past in this room; to everyone who ever lived here. And it's the pigeons connecting us to all of that.'

Pigeons flying through dark tunnelled time. They both look out, see this one pigeon now, fluttering across rooftops. Mauvish shape against slate and stone, unreal.

MEDUSA

L AS RAMBLAS SUMMERTIME NIGHT. Are you there now, standing up on the chair because of the beetles, that charm bracelet on your upheld arm slipping down towards the elbow? That's the way I'll always think of you. Two great flying beetles have settled on the floor of your room—the window's been left open due to the heat, but you hadn't pictured an invasion. I should've thought a woman such as yourself would have seen them off. You tell me you hardly ever manage to sleep, and when you do you never close your eyes.

In the Barcelona morning I watch her pass me on the way to her day's fixed position, her little box-top from which she views the world. Lady of the Twining Snakes, with skin and cloth all silvered over, all the same texture, just as a statue would be. Silver-shiny, convincing *Modernista*, only a bit prettier than they need to be, because you can't totally alienate the coin-givers. She *is* a statue, then she comes to life. Look. It's a show of feeling activated by money, otherwise she'd still be mute. Money's the only thing which moves her. Shock of the prosaic in a world of dream. You start off being dismayed, then remind yourself she needs to survive, the same as anybody—she's not an enchantress who can live on air. At the end of the day the real person goes home, removes her make-up, is vulnerable, cannot sleep.

Colonnade of human flesh, pretending to be stone or metal imitating life. I'm walking along the line, through the avenue of silent figures on boxes. A bluff toy soldier with a key in his back, a clockwork imitation. *Turn me.* Again, a matter of money in the slot. And a Roman centurion all bronze in his pleats and breastplate, and a clown. There's a little shower of coins and one of them starts to activate—a ghost, tip tilted and shivering in his sheet. A languid grey ghost to make us gasp. For a few seconds he's coming at us with sheeted arms uplifted, with a hollow stare. There's a moaning sound, a whooshing as of a soul in torment. People stop on the walkway, they point and laugh. It *is* amazing. And then all goes empty as if the breath has been extinguished, as if the button of final destiny has been pressed. No matter what point was reached when it happened, this will be the new eternity till the next time. If no more coins come, the hand will be held out at that agonised angle forever. 'Let's have another go,' someone says. But it's hard to read what's really going on with these human statues, what's being offered and taken, so much seems to rest on the make-up and the outfits. The silver woman with snakes coiled up on her head doesn't move, no money has fallen into her basket. I've walked past but then I turn back. *I think I'll go for it.*

She's all writhing and twirling in snake-like motion as though she's influenced by what's on her head. There's a sudden burning anguish, a snarl and a glaring eye for you, for your trouble, a wild thrusting out of hands, as if they'd like to throttle you; an impersonation of emotional disturbance. The charm bracelet on her arm clinkles like a wind chime. But the eyes of the Snake Lady do not register the audience even when she's moving. They're the dark centre of her, looking only at what they want to see.

Another hour and she's saying to her neighbour, 'Home time.' He's a birdman in a beaked mask, too drugged up just now to notice that she's off. She jumps down from the box, doing this last public act with style. But when she's on the ground the smile leaves her, she's taken it on board she's invisible now. Her head itches with the heat and the sponge-filled snakes, though she's not unhappy in her work, there's a buzz to it that gives her a good feeling. Her ugliness has power, her pretend ugliness. What she has to do is make the audience afraid to look at her but still pop the money in, still need to see more. It's a double game. She catches a reflection of her silver self in a shop window across the way, thinks fleetingly of the cycle of perpetual resurrection. From stillness, to

MEDUSA

movement and back. It's the rhythm of her working life. But later, at home, she wipes away the paint, her skin's no longer silver, more a muddy rose.

Siesta Saturday. I see them at Parc Guell, hand-in-hand. She is snakeless. By the way, how does she manage to have snakes like that, so realistic, so curling over and leaping up with that twist to the tails? Hard to imagine they're not really growing out of her head and she's quite ordinary. I blink when she comes into view. Without her box and apparatus you wouldn't glance twice at her. Up the steep-winding road they've come, the hand-in-hand lovers, a little out of breath because they're getting on a bit and the heat is something else.

She lives in my apartment block, her lover comes round sometimes. It's a furtive business and he'll never quite look at you. I see him now and again, always acting as if it's a secret that he's there. All that evasion and yet everybody knows, especially the wife. It's common knowledge she's sharpening her knives in readiness. Concita, anxious but resistant, sits it out. On occasion I see her in the hallway, we never speak.

The lovers are to be seen from time to time; *when* can't be predicted. Today, up in Parc Güell, she's twining her body like a serpent or a dragon, the light twinkling across her as though she's some mosaic replica. Wine is drunk, the lovers, besotted, roll around on the grass. *Possessed*, or about to be. I pass them as they clink glasses out in the toohot day. Why are they here? I interpret it as a need for their union to be sealed by scorching, as if they've made a pact which demands to be forcibly sworn. This sun is the chosen god of consecration, denial at last denied. Lapping up this sun, Bacchic and extravagant, they do not notice me, or anything. Her room, the late night beetles are so far off.

But still, it's hard to really think in terms of *them*. Her natural state seems to be standing up on her performance-box, motionless and then sporadically uncoiling. Her snake-lady image is a totally singles thing and I can't really picture her as part of a couple—even an illicit parttime couple would not be *her*. The Snake Lady always stands alone, she's someone you have to pay to see in action. She's a one-woman show with

GOD OF THE PIGEONS

a *Look at me; Look away when I tell you*, authority, everybody absolutely knowing they're only here to witness what she chooses, nothing more. Just the shadow perhaps, of what she might really be, an after-glow.

I see her hanging out her washing on the yellow balcony. There's a line of rope with coat hangers balanced along it, stopped from slipping by pegs. Concita, in her mauve satin slip dips down, attaching another peg. I see her because the building has an indentation. There's a little gully between us, our balconies are facing. She has a pink geranium on her stone sill, today she waters it sloppily, spilling much.

Las Ramblas summertime day. Concita of the Twining Snakes. I throw a coin into her little metallic basket. She twirls in a hard hearted, unrelenting way today that makes you want to see more because of that bite it has to it. There's some strange energy that you want to get to the bottom of; it draws you. She stops. You haven't seen enough. But another coin wouldn't do it, you realise sadly. More and more coins, you'd still be nowhere. She starts, she stops. She takes you in the same small circle, a ferocity in her eyes which isn't quite explained, an anger in her curving arms. You want to know more, she will not tell. You definitely have the intuition she never will. The red-coated soldier is marching sedately on the spot as the Snake Lady twines, the key in his back turning as he rotates. He is slow and hesitant as though nearing some ambivalent end. His smile remains jaunty though, refusing to be subdued by the constraints of money and time. Then click click, the two figures stop in unison, as though it's a routine, some pre-arranged clever trick of timing. The soldier's wound down to nothing, the smile on his lips frozen, like some crazy man who can't let go even though the moment's past. Concita has thrown her arms forward in a last gesture of going somewhere, even if it's only to fool you. You feel a sense of alarm, as though there's a particular place she's really trying to get to and is prevented merely by circumstance. Click, one arm is held up over her head like a Spanish dancer, the other beckons. But where? In the Avenue of Moving Statues the money tinkles into tins, there's a semblance of

MEDUSA

humans coming suddenly to life; then all too soon the life force departs needing to be resurrected—there's such a look on each blank face which says, *Help me, help me. Give me life.* And you can make all the movement happen with your fingertips; with your generosity. What a power they give you. The Laughing Sailor is now quite still at the end of the line. How he'll duck and wheel and do himself in with laughter for a few loose coins. He's beetroot faced from all the putting out and the hope, and from booze and the sun of over-bright days. More power to your fingertips and your casual thrown coins.

Concita as Hermione, stepping down from her box gracefully. *Look I'm alive now, I'm really real.* And the wife waits, waits by the corners of buildings, shadowed at midday, spills tears into her tall iced drinks by night. There are always knives at the ready in her heart. Spreading the word, spreading her fury at betrayal. Has it in for the Snake Lady with all her charms. Sees blood, sees only blood, for miles and miles in all and everything.

In the central hallway of the flats I hear a sound. I'm making for my apartment, am here unexpectedly because I'm a fast and quiet walker. It's a quarter to one, I've drunk too much. The stairway shimmers but even so, I see what is to be seen quite clearly, I see the man lurking aimlessly, not wanting to be present, or not wanting to be visible. He doesn't look at me, as if that will make either of those conditions attainable. I smile as I climb the stairs. I'd like to say to him, 'But everybody knows. Why bother to hide now, you might as well relax, enjoy what is.' I say nothing, of course, just pass him, fitting in with his need to be unacknowledged. I want to laugh but I think of his anguish and the wasted energy and instead I sigh. Mid-morning here is Concita with her watering can. Did nobody tell her you shouldn't water plants when the sun's shining?

Out later with the buskers and the jugglers and the cup-and-balls magicians I see her twined snakes' head. She's fresh today, she attracts customers. When she's still there's a kind of majesty to her, when she's twirling there's fire. She's raking the money in with her stoppings and startings—some days in a life are like this, little compartments of success. She looks happy in her contrived ugliness. I know that later she and the lover will go up to Parc Guell, will trudge their way hand-in-hand up the steep winding road and then the steps, that she'll then find the energy to dance exuberantly, dramatically, before the mosaic dragon on the summit, and her charm bracelet will tinkle and jangle against her arm. At last, they'll disappear into the surrounding bushes, there will be groans and sighs. Her hair will be more than ordinary now, you won't be afraid to look at her when she comes out dishevelled, half laughing, smoothing out her skirt.

A mid-week night. Concita comes running out of her apartment door as I climb the stairs. She calls to me as if we're used to speaking, as though it's something we always do and it isn't the case she's usually furtive and hidden with a look of not wanting to be disturbed. And to me too, it feels very natural, as though we are after all on chatting terms. I can talk to her quite easily it seems, yet be afraid at the same time of looking her in the eye. She's in her Medusa outfit, the snake headdress gesticulating in a menacing way.

'The beetles!' she cries out, jumping back to her door and holding it open for me to go inside. We pass through a dingy kitchen with archaic and macabre-looking cooking equipment hanging up on the walls from hooks. A rusty grater, a knife sharpener which I can't believe would ever work, a knife with a long tapered blade which looks as though it doesn't need it. I feel a chill and wonder if I'm afraid. In a terracotta room with candlelight and a dark bed in one corner, I see the creatures, surprisingly large and scuttling, very much alive. Her casement window is open, a frail curtain flapping slightly against its frame. Concita screams and the beetles zoom under the bed. It takes quite a while for them to come out again. During the time we cannot see them, I hold her hand and form a plan, which she's too jittery to listen to. I'd noticed a large tin on a shelf above the draining board as we'd come through the narrow kitchen. We go back there, hand-in-hand tightly, and I fetch this tin down—yes, it's empty. And then I find a kitchen board. When the beetles come sidling out again I get the tin over them. There's a desperate scuffling and then silence. Concita's up on a chair wailing in a muted voice, her shoulders hunched, her arms raised up, the snake headdress casting pointed shadows all around. But maybe they're not menacing, only jester-like. I fix my mind on bells and tassels and try to hang onto this image as I slide the board underneath the tin, bit by bit. I unthink the snakes and change the shadows into other things, the room to other places. Finally, when I've tipped the beetles out of the tall, grand windows, Concita and I sip nightcaps, watch the beginnings of the dawn. I see a tissue on her dressing table with some make-up on one corner. She'd been about to remove her mask when the beetles had flown in.

I'm driving up into the mountains and uncannily, keep seeing the lovers. A hot afternoon. I stop at the roadside, buy a basket of fruit, look back over the red-poppy plains. I see the lovers in their fish-silver car go gliding upwards. A film-star car with mirrored glass. Later, when I pass one of the packing stations, I see the pair of them sitting on a rustic bench eating peaches. *Los Melocotonés* in white paper hats. Crossing a bridge near de la Verge de Montserrat, I catch sight of them again, entwined in that way they have, staring down at some quick running stream. They're kind of oblivious, not caring now who is noticing them and who isn't. They are people of extremes. Concita wears a straw hat with a brim so wide I cannot see her face. I guess she's pensive, that the sight of the fast flowing water gives her no joy, makes her think only of loss, of what can't be held onto. Or maybe I think that afterwards, when I realise that this was the last time I ever saw her. Sight of the woven straw hat, a little straggly at the edges, cutting her off at the neck.

It's moving towards late summer, people are leaving Barcelona like migrating birds, whole flocks of them going somewhere, I'm not sure where. There's a bustle in the flats, Concita's balcony is full of objects. I notice particularly a birdcage without a bird, and a vanity case, both pegged to the single rope. When somebody shifts the casement they jiggle like puppets. It's mid-morning, there's a smell of coffee and toast. Music flares out tinnily across the gully between the buildings, followed by radiochat. Sense of things happening, sense of change; when I go out the hallway is thick with belongings. People rush in and out of doors, claiming things, removing them. Spaces are filled up immediately with somebody else's stuff. Concita's will have been some of these because later on, her balcony is empty and there's a gone-forever feel to it. The pink geranium, how did she pack that? Was it left behind? I can't see it anywhere.

The lover of Concita struggles in mid-day sun across La Rambla de los Caputxins, a suitcase in either hand. The man is rattled, almost colliding with the popcorn seller, attracting abuse. He slips at last down a side street. Gone then, like an unanswered question, a story only guessed at vaguely and then lost. Quite a few of the human statues have also gone, there are wider gaps between the boxes. No sign of the bluff toy soldier now, he's packed his bags for somewhere or other and left. The beaky birdman is still here, hovering hawk-like when the coins are thrown to him, as though to swoop. I get the feeling you're a mouse to him, or a smaller weaker bird. I stroll along feeling restless, deprived of conclusions. City of mosaic and lacy stone, surreal and serpentine, how could Concita leave? I suppose a woman like herself is at home practically anywhere, yet I guess that she'll be back. Unconsciously I'm already searching though I can't see her and there's nothing at all to say she was ever here. At a café table near La Sagrada Familia I sit and watch the faces of remaining tourists. Have they looked and been smitten, or been struck? I search their eyes for clues.

I'm at a loose end now, on the look out for signs. I read in the paper of a severed head washed up on the shoreline and am sure it's her, convinced it has to be. No body ever comes to light and the most shocking thing is that the head itself simply disappears. It's been stolen from police custody, or been lost and so can't be investigated. This compounds things for me, I'm sure it's the head of Concita. There's no mention of snakes in the newspaper report, but why would there be? The snakes were just her working gear—she had to pay the rent, like everybody else. I stroll the close to autumn streets hoping to catch sight of her but

MEDUSA

knowing it won't happen. At Placa Reial I imagine for a second I've just caught up with her at a metallic table, applying silvered make-up like in the old days. If I could see Concita one more time I'd be a happy man. To see her coming to life for money, throwing out sinuous arms in a wild embrace of air and then turning still, her act over till the next time—it would be enough. I go home at twilight, thinking suddenly of Antonio Gaudí in his ragged clothes with a peanut in his pocket, or one peseta, seeing it's impossible to really know such things as this when the moment's past. Could have been either, both or neither. Hit by a trolley bus, a tram. Where had he been looking the moment before it happened, what was he thinking of? Was he considering the properties of stone? Thinking of Gaudi dying unexpectedly, thinking of the night beetles and Concita high above me on her chair. Another time I believe I see the wife of Concita's lover with a dangerous looking man. He could have done it, cut off her head like that, done it at that woman's prompting. She looks like a woman who would prompt. But when I look back I don't see them, nor any turning they might have taken, perhaps I'm going mad. Like the statues I should get out of here. The summer has been hot and long, time to go now, maybe that's always what it comes to.

On windy nights I hear the tinkle of your bracelet, the charms falling against one another as you raise your arms. *If you look back at me you're a dead man*, your voice says, so I do not do it, I know now it's time to let you go. I've come up to the waterfront, gaze down and see reflections. A winged horse, a mermaid, a crescent moon.

SQUEEZE

2004:
In his new flat in clear sunny light, in all the fresh space of it, Joel lies on his bed in the biggest room, lies on his king-size bed smoking a cigarette, later he is going to build shelves. Planks of wood stand heaped together in the middle of the floor, and sometimes fall, and have to be stacked up again, as though for a bonfire. Maybe he won't build anything after all. Mmm, maybe he won't, he doesn't have to, it's up to him, doesn't have to have shelves, things can go anywhere, can go on the floor. Between the cairns of clothes which are already piling up there, though he will be hanging them up, but he hasn't yet, because he doesn't have hangers or a wardrobe, or a rail. He smiles to himself feeling happy, in his new space, where he can have things just as he wants them, where he doesn't have to bother, just for the sake of it, if he doesn't want to, doesn't have to get bogged down by domestic stuff. It doesn't have to be tidy, in his space, he doesn't need it to be, feels beyond a need like that. He's lying on his bed, feeling great, drawing on his cigarette. Scatters of ash trail to duvet, to floor.

2005:
Here on his bed in the biggest room, with the stacks of wood, a small rag of a rug, a three legged chair on which no one could sit, poised at a tip tilt angle, precarious in the sea of discarded clothes. Joel feeling some satisfaction that he has let things be, that he doesn't have an urge to tidy up, to make shelves, can accept things just as they are, haphazard, be like this. Feels a sense of superiority, seeing the junky bits, and the scraps and scrits, is reminded how he's above it all, and he has this great

sense of peace inside him, because his place is the way he wants it, he can pick his way, through scattered paper, be amused seeing the spread of disorder, he himself at the centre of everything, the ordered one, the unchaotic principle, ruling the space, choosing to let it be, to not be hampered by domestic considerations, liking, yes liking, things the way they are. But there's the suggestion of a shadow.

2006:
Joel has moved to the master bedroom, just slightly smaller, still a good size though, big enough, it's only that he was feeling a bit lost where he was, and a little crowded out. It's better here, he doesn't need that much space, sitting in his double bed, smoking and dreaming. The ash scatters. He's feeling happy, noticing dust on the blue carpet, obscuring the outlines of the blue roses that he doesn't like that much anyway, on the carpet which was already here when he moved into the flat, and he's facing a gas cooker standing sideways on, at the end of the bed, feels a pride. It's all fallen into place, around him. Lying in bed, seeing the cooker, with its splashes of grease, stains of the splashes from the days when the cooker was in use. Now the cooker just stands there, doesn't have a function, it pleases him, like the stacks of wood in the sitting room now that he's not bothering with shelves, like the rusty iceskates speckled blades up, in their little stack. The cooker and the wood and the skates are not in the way, nothing is in the way here, everything has its place-not-place. He's allowed all of this to happen, which indicates he has a kind of power, exercises total control, over the realm of the meaningless. There's a cup and a broken jug lying sideways together, just together, right under the window, by the wall where he has left them, like a Still Life, nice aesthetic accident. He likes that. But a slight shadow, there's a slight shadow, he wants it to go away.

2007:
Lying on the double bed, in the master bedroom, won't go out today, he's too tired, and he's happy enough where he is, all considered. Sees a

snag in the curtain, knows he's been looking at it for some time, doesn't know when it got there, or how it got there but who cares, the whole place is full of snags one way and another, he's not fazed by this. Lights up a cigarette, puffs out into the room, sees the stained side of the old gas cooker, the snag, the snags, dust on the bedstead. Ash. Still proud of his achievements he is, here, in this space, his kind of living museum of the freedom of the will, but, there's the shadow. The shadow of a suspicion that things are not quite what he wants them to be after all, there is this difficulty he hadn't thought of. To do with the light. He doesn't know why it is but there's a kind of greyish look in the room, a darkening, whereas he'd prefer it bright, it *should* be light in here, the window's facing south. Yawn. He's going to get up and open the curtains, in a bit he is, after he's had a little nap he will.
Shadow.

2008:
Spare bedroom, a single bed. Neat and tidy feel to it—Joel feels like being contained, can't seem to take the bigger space. He lies on the bed, nearly takes up the whole of it, nothing to spare, there's not a lot of space in this room and what there is is occupied. To go out he has to walk carefully between bales of piled newspapers—he's always been one for reading the papers and can't ever bring himself to throw any of em away. Still, they're good as soundproofing, good for keeping the place warm, and where there's no papers there's the motorbike parts, from when he had the bike, the car door, from when he had the car. In the many newspapers there's all that information which he might use, in another life he might, if he could have another life, and leave this one behind. The bike and the car parts, if they were attached to a frame, had an engine, were part of a machine which worked, could be the vehicles of his removal. To somewhere else. No, what's he saying? None of the stuff has to have a use, does it. He reminds himself. Stares out at the flaking walls, and the peeling paint on the door and the brown stains from four years of cigarette smoke puffed out on a constant basis. It's

SQUEEZE

okay, he's not a slave to domestic tidiness, that's something, that's an important thing. When he thinks of the energy other people put in to seeing to their places it makes him tired. He's free of all of that stuff, his time's his own. But the shadow's got darker.

2009:
The shadow is intense, he can't bear the sight of it. The pitted silver of hub caps—from when he had the motor—shine out at him, seeming cynical, he doesn't want to see them. They look like hostile eyeballs, gloating over his discomfort. Joel lights up a cigarette, tries to get relaxed. He draws in slowly, blows out resoundingly. But he still feels disconcerted, can't help thinking of how the grey smoke puffs will turn brown, cling to the room, become a component of the decay which he no longer wishes to see. It's part of the shadow, definitely part of the shadow, but he needs to smoke, he can't stop doing it. Shit, he's losing control! He feels oppressed in other ways as well now. The things, they seem to bear down on him, the bike parts, the car parts, slicing into him with the strength and viciousness of metal. He feels cut, this makes him draw more heavily on his cigarette, this depresses him. The room is small, but not small enough. Once the decay had represented freedom of choice, but now... The idea of picture frames without any pictures, some still waiting to be mended, this says it all. It's a torture to him to contemplate let alone see, he needs to get out.

2010:
Life in the cupboard. Life is dark, the advantage with this being that he can't now see the shadow. Even so, there's this feeling of oppression. All the things in the flat, now he can't see them seem to be bearing down on him at a faster rate. He imagines them bouncing out at him through the dark, a tyranny of objects. The broken furniture, the wood, the ice skates, the empty picture frames, the snag and the snags, the old gas cooker, the bike parts from when he had the bike, the car parts from when he had the car, the dust, the chunky piles of paper. It's as if they're

all now pressing down, crushing him, altogether they are much much bigger than he is, and he's afraid to move in case they crash right down on top of him. He's almost afraid to breathe, in case he dislodges something and starts an avalanche of all the junk. Not that there's any room to move, in the cupboard.

Funny, it's the last place he'd have thought of ending up, it's the last place he wants to be, but he's here, he's here anyway, somehow, you'd hardly call it a choice. It's just that one thing leads to another and you can't help it, he couldn't help it. Moving in this one direction to this very tiny space where he feels the impossibility of everything, where he lies quite still so's not to upset the status quo, and if he has to go out, to the loo or anywhere, he can hardly get to the door anyway, because it's so cramped in here, he's so hemmed in, he tries wriggling sideways, tries to flatten himself against the wall as he goes, it's a *squeeze*.

MIMOSA, HOUSE OF DREAM

IN MY DREAM WORLD it's only ever Jamie and me, and I'm locked inside it now. But suddenly seeing Romilly draws me out of my little reverie, and I start getting critical, asking myself what the two of us get out of pretending to be in love the way we do. Romilly's at the station again today with her suitcase, her hair now startling, vivid as orange peel, her face stark toothpaste white. The orange kicks your mind away, the white brings it back with a question mark. Jamie says Romilly is older than she seems and is afraid of looking faded. There's a small wan smile on her face, she's asking for help. But quietly, discretely, she'll understand if no one's got the time. Who could turn her down? Romilly, a waitress in a cyberpunk café is a tenant of Mimosa—a house we share together. She's not going anywhere that *I* know of. This stunt at the railway station is some kind of little routine.

Skyla, who's at college with me in the City though in a different department, is another of my house-sharers. Compared with Romilly she's quite open about where she is in life. At least she started off that way. When her mother died, Skyla went downwards into caves. She explained she wanted to taste the earth and hole herself up in soft darkness to soothe the pain away. She was looking for something down there but she wasn't sure what, maybe just the darkness itself. And she said there was a silence beyond what you could imagine if you hadn't ever been caving. She was satisfied with the terror she felt. Her mother's name was Dolores and, sorrowfully, she'd died some years ago when Skyla was barely twelve. So, Skyla said, she was an orphan. Her eyes looked tragic. She told me this the first day when she was bringing her stuff in, looking up at the string of light bulbs in the hall as if the place was too bright for comfort. Dolores, dolour, sadness. Skyla, sky, out there, think blue and higher than the world. She wanted to challenge that, didn't feel like living up to her name she told me. And then Dane her boyfriend, moved in, and the talk dried up.

Dane was silent as one of those caves Skyla used to climb down into, and I imagine that's why she liked him; he was silent even when he was doing his Glam Rock Star impersonations. He'd mouth the words of songs, throwing back his body from hip to shoulder to indicate how loud and raucous, how uncontained, the sound should be, but no real noise would ever come out from between his lips. I remembered how I'd sung hymns silently when I was in junior school assembly and wondered if Dane felt like I did then. Too embarrassed to hear the sound of my own voice, shocked if a little squeak of it flared out unexpectedly. Not wanting to know it was there, even a whisper. Was it like this for Dane when he rocked around up there in their room those late weekend nights?

I wondered whether this Rock Star figure was the real Dane, rather than the Dane we thought we knew. And though he may not be quite able to draw out of himself what, deep down, he was sure he was, he still had to play this part every now and again to keep his life on track.

Soon Skyla turned into somebody every bit as silent as Dane himself. If you came across the two of them in the house they'd stand back against the wall to let you pass, even if it was on the stairway, as if trying to be invisible, as if they feared contamination. Resentment simmered in them. Their smudge-black kohl-smothered eyes.

Neil and Jamie, in the big double room at the front, had a cat. They didn't tell me, but I saw it sitting up by their window one day, its teeth on edge because of bird movement in the tree outside. 'You've got to let that cat out,' I told them. Jamie said he didn't think Neil would be happy with that as he'd be worried. He said Neil had always played the part of father to the cat. I said that a cat likes to roam around but Neil disagreed, it was

MIMOSA, HOUSE OF DREAM

that sort of cat. It liked a quiet domestic life and that was that. Neil said he'd observed it long enough and he could vouch for this being the case. Neil's sharp steely eyes glinted as he said this, he was a lecturer and could easily get pissed off at being told what to do by a mere student, but still he brought the cat out from the room where it had been stowed away like a cushion on the seat by the window. The cat had no claws, Neil told me proudly. They'd been plucked out so it wouldn't scratch the furniture. Neil and even Jamie looked at me with challenging eyes as though I'd been about to claim their cat had ripped up the rag of carpet in the hall or shredded the strip of greasy kitchen curtain.

'So, maybe,' Jamie said, 'we shouldn't let it go in the garden. Maybe the cat will be attacked.' The two of them stood there grieving for the cat, whose name was Lemur, as though it was a different kind of animal from what it was. The first thing the cat did once it got out there was catch a mouse. Neil and Jamie looked on with disbelief as the cat let the mouse run under the kitchen chair, as it gave a wiggle and then a pounce. Their cat, their precious Lemur cat, was doing this. Neil was someone who despised competitive sports and any act of violence on principle. Now, against all his hopes and expectations, his cat had turned out to be a thoroughly vicious type. On the other hand, as Jamie put it later, the cat was Neil's only child.

Ken came in and said it was cruel and Neil and Jamie agreed it was. But Neil's eyes were full of unstoppable pride as if his only child had beaten all the other children in a race; his feelings of fatherhood were stronger than his disapproval. By now, his lips were dry with anxiety because the mouse had been able to get away in time, thus denying Lemur its rightful chance. Then all at once the mouse ran out from under the chair and the cat chased it to the cupboard. Neil was quivering with paternal joy and Ken started swearing at him.

'What's he like?' went Ken.

Then next minute the cat had pounced and the mouse had been right there and the cat had caught it. It was in the cat's mouth, and then somehow it was out again and running and it was plain for all to see that

GOD OF THE PIGEONS

Neil was practically having a seizure, but Ken got the mouse away from the cat and put it outside and Neil's body drooped with the sense of anticlimax because his child had been deprived of happiness. He lowered his eyes in disappointment for Lemur and Jamie looked disappointed too, though only out of loyalty.

'Imagine our Lemur catching a mouse,' droned Neil, once the fire had faded out of him, in his usual grating voice.

And it was clear that even though Lemur challenged his ideals, Neil had too much fatherly regard for the animal to whisper a word against it.

Ken was the other house sharer. Like Skyla and Dane, he kept very much to himself and went in and out of his door quickly if you were in the hallway, and that was because his room was like a rat's nest. It was his private place of infestation. Ken was neat and reasonable, but his room was a desperate den of filth, with food remains piling up in the centre. Meaty stuff and old takeaways, bones and shrivelled chicken skin, all mouldy. He wanted it the way it was or he didn't have the energy to change things. But he didn't want anybody else to see. And Ken was in his room most of the time. He must've sat in there and torn up strips of paper for hours on end, because afterwards when he left, that's the main thing you saw there. A huge ball of grubby paper shreds. It was his nest. Jamie said Ken lived as if he was a rat and that's why he'd had so much sympathy for the mouse Lemur had caught. When Ken moved out, Karin came. Jamie and I did a mega cleaning job on the room and Karin moved in for a few months. She was pregnant and had taken the room here to be anonymous. She wouldn't tell any of us where she came from, but she kind of made too much of a deal out of it as if we were all pestering her for details of her normal life. It wasn't that way in the least, but all the same she acted as if that's what was going on. Sometimes I'd see her down by the front door waiting for the odd, occasional letter, afraid, no doubt that somebody else would see it first and try and decipher the postmark. One night when Karin got pissed she told me her sister Tina was going to have her baby and it would be brought up as the child of Tina and Brian, Tina's husband. She, Karin, the real mother, was going to pretend to be the aunt. The child would never know; they would keep up the act for a whole lifetime. Karin didn't say the word *deception*. She just said it would be better for everybody if they all kept quiet about it and she'd learned a way of organising everything so's nobody could ever find out. The only thing she didn't tell me was why they were doing it. Karin became very friendly with Neil and Jamie. Jamie used to get her strawberries when summer came and Neil let Lemur go in and sit on Karin's bed. Karin was slim for a long time then all at once she got very pregnant looking. At last one day she disappeared, leaving a note. She'd had the baby she said and now had to go back to her sister's. We phoned all the local maternity wards and they said they'd never heard of her.

'But wait a minute', said Neil, 'did we know her name? Did anybody know what Karin's surname was; was her first name even Karin?'

How could she have had the baby just like that, so silently? And who helped Karin move her stuff?

'She didn't have any stuff,' said Neil. 'When you come to think of it.' Neil said she could have faked the pregnancy with a pillow. That we had to take on board there were people all around us who were pretending to be something they were not. We may not know *why* they did it, but it was important to be aware it was going on.

So the room was vacant again and that was when the man moved in who thought he should have been born as a reindeer. Well, that was more or less what he told me and Jamie one night when he came and joined us at the kitchen table where we were sitting together sharing this dish of ice cream. He confessed it calmed him to think of a reindeer and imagine himself with that same strong and graceful body. He particularly liked the idea of having a reindeer's antlers. His eyes fixed on us and glowed distant at one and the same time, which for all I knew was standard reindeer behaviour. He was in close up and a mile away all in the same breath; there and not there. The guy's name was Alan and I could tell he'd fit in really well and be a popular member of the house in no time. Which was one of the things that led me to ponder what in hell's name I myself was doing here.

When Romilly came in I introduced her to Alan the Ungulate. Her hair, I noticed then, was much more orange than it used to be. She did one of her wan smiles at Alan and he looked quite keen to know her better.

'Hi there,' he went, doing a soft ungulate shuffle of the feet.

Alan said later he thought Jamie and I were a couple. That doesn't surprise me, I'm quite aware of the way we both try to create that effect though I haven't yet analysed what it's really about. Newcomers are always taken in. Alan wasn't somebody who was disinclined to talk. Even though he had nothing whatever to say, he could spin out enough banal repetitions to last through a whole evening. The pits were when he'd go, 'Hi there', every time he came back into a room after being absent only a minute or two.

'Why is the house called Mimosa?' Alan asked, his first night.

'Because there's a mimosa tree at the back which is a dominant feature. It's tall, with great spiky branches, in the Spring it has these clusters of yellow flowers,' said Neil, who knows all kinds of facts like this. 'The interesting thing about a Mimosa is . . .' Neil went on to add, but Romilly cut him short hastily, as if she for one didn't care to hear. We'd all switched off, I suppose, even the Ungulate, as Neil can be quite tedious when he puts his lecturer's voice on, so we never did find out.

So here's Romilly with her hair the brightest yet and deathly pale, with this suitcase, and for a laugh I'd go over and ask her if she's really going somewhere, except for the fact she's chatting to this couple. She looks as if she's asking them for help. They're both smiling so whatever she wants must be okay. I go and stand by this magazine rack in time to hear Romilly tell them she's just come out of hospital, and then they move away a bit and what with a few intervening noises I don't get to find out any more. The three of them are moving off towards the exit and without stopping to think what excuse I'll make if Romilly happens to see me, I follow along behind. We all get out to the street and I realise

MIMOSA, HOUSE OF DREAM

Romilly's playing the part of a convalescent, the man's carrying her case and she's between the man and the woman, gripping onto an arm of each. I ask myself if Romilly *has* been in hospital. She is looking totally ashen, it's true, but more in the style of a mime artiste than an invalid, I would have said. The trio go slowly across the road, Romilly doing a good hobbling simulation, and I see them walk over to the swishest, most upmarket apartment block in sight. Here goodbyes are said, and Romilly gives the couple a kiss that's not threatening but flattering on account of her being older than the wife is and also humble. The couple look happy and wave goodbyes as they leave. Romilly climbs up the marble steps to the door of the apartments. I hang about awhile suspecting she'll come out again pretty quickly and I'm right. After five or so minutes have gone by I see her pointed chin and then the white masque of the rest of her face peeking out with caution. After ten, she's back on the pavement and trotting off in the direction of Mimosa. I go home too. The phone in the hall is ringing as I open the front door and when I pick up the receiver this woman answers who says her name is Dolores and she's trying to get hold of her daughter, Skyla. Do I know her? She'd been away in Patagonia she tells me, but now she's back. Has she got the right number? Could I get Skyla to give her a call?

Skyla herself is outside in the garden, Neil informs me with a funny look when I make enquiries in the kitchen. It turns out he's absolutely right. Skyla's digging a hole, apparently she's been out there all the afternoon. We go and see how she's getting on, she's down to her waist by now. She's sweating and straining and tipping out bucket after bucket of semi-hard Spring earth with no letting up, her face with a bereaved look. But if it's a grave she's digging, where's the corpse? No sign of Dane, but it's soon revealed why not. Jamie and the Ungulate come and join us and we all look up at Skyla's room as there's a strange sound coming from it. The lights up there are full on even though it isn't dark yet and the window's open. There's a harsh and blatant zang, zang, zanging going on and the occasional slap on wood. Dane is doing his impersonation of a Glam Rock Star, with a shiny guitar he has no idea how to play. He's holding the neck of this guitar up towards some unseen audience as though begging for masturbation. We see his face stretched and orgasmic, his roaring lips from which no sound comes. While his girlfriend, down here in the garden, digs and digs like the clappers, as though she's trying to get away from him and all of us, as though she's trying to reach the dark.

I see that Neil was right about the tree as well. It's a mass of yellow flowers now. Quite beautiful, I suppose. I'm suddenly aware that Neil's talking to somebody and I see it's Lemur who's come out too, keen to be in on the latest bit of action. Although my ears refuse to believe it straight away, I'm sure I hear Neil call him 'son'. Then Jamie bounds over and the two of us start dancing as if there's real live music coming from up in Skyla's room and soon we're doing our 'lost to the world' act together. I'm only experimenting to find out how it would feel to be like this; to be quite other than how I really am. But we're putting on a brilliant show. It's just as if we're a pair of lovers, the way we're eye-locked, the way we can't let go. There again perhaps I *really* am what I think I'm only pretending to be. But I don't have to worry too much; in Mimosa anything goes. Everybody who passes through this place is living these kinds of experiments. None of us may quite know why, but in a dreamworld this is how you are.

LITTLE ELVA

Hedges dark and sharp. He can't remember, doesn't remember seeing them, on the way down. He's used to the road but can't picture hedges like this, so angular they look, and fierce. *Can* imagine the presence of an army teetering there, edge of the road, where is he? Okay, keep calm, it's familiar, he knows where he is, doesn't he? Yes, but, but there's a difference, plus the lights. It's the lights making the hedges seem like enemies. As if he's in another world now. Dart of sweat on his eyelid, brow, in the strait of flesh between nose and lip, and his tongue comes out, licks upwards, *higher* than the lip, trying to stop a tickle. He blinks his eyes. Lights, lights getting brighter, now *so* bright and seeming to hang above his head. Like lanterns, like bloody lanterns. There's this roar to them, or not *to them* but there is a roar. It's in his ears but coming from somewhere else, loudest thing. In his ears and in the road, and by the hedges. The hedges, fuck it. James, who hardly swears, has swearing torn out of him by the sharp outlines of the hedges, they're that menacing, and by the roar. Only way of coping, seems to be. His eyes dilate. Little Elva, these lights have gone through the stages. Saucers, soup-plates, millwheels. Like the eyes of magical dogs there's no stopping em from getting bigger and bigger. He dreams he's in the bottom of a hollow tree, unexpectedly there's a lit-up hall inside and rooms rich with money chests, nothing rough about the place as you might've imagined in the abstract. He'd like a fag, quick, he needs one but hasn't got a match, and can't do fuck all about his brow sweat, it's trickling into his eye, no stopping it and the blinding light is everywhere, and then the dark. Darkest. Little Elva the world's gone upside down.

GOD OF THE PIGEONS

Hell though, the sexiest thing, Little Elva in her slinky sizzle of a dress, it's Christmas, she's partied herself up, all shimmer and shoulder straps and dancing the way she can, look at me now dear, look at me, no don't, *don't* you hear, changed me mind. You'd only worry girl, hate to see those worry lines streaking down between your eyes, making you frown, and your mouth going the same direction all weight at the corners, and you'd get a tear. Don't you cry now, no not that. Elva the ice-white bride and then the going away outfit, that flowerblue velvet cloche she wore. Forget-me-not, but I know she never would. *Just you think of it, will do you good, girl.* And *Viva Italia*, the pearly-white smile you gave me, and here we were in Genoa looking up relations on your mother's mother's side, and in Sorrento, on your mother's father's, then later in Barcelona looking up relations, on your dad's.

Concentrate on that. Elva your eyes all aflash, let me see you, *always* see you that way, nothing less because I can't bear it either. I'll be crinkly laughter, you a mocking stare, but upturned at the edges, please for that. Can't take anything less than uptilted, can't manage anything bad, and we don't have to 'cause isn't it true to say that we're the lucky ones? When I first saw you your eyes black as night cats, couldn't believe there were such eyes as yours, till I saw you standing by the mantle shelf at that party where we met. Knew I'd have to have you, you were mine, you must be mine, such eyes as that, they held me. I was yours but would you have me? Well, you did. Now you'll be home, watching telly I should think, or listening to music, you won't be looking at the clock and wondering where I am because I'm not late yet, but funny thing, I'm here, on this bloody road as it turns out, and you can't see me, but thank the Lord for that.

The swirl of upside down, madness of not knowing where the sky is, or the ground, then there's a hard flat something, and *that* must be the ground, knocking the breath out of me, the shock of it. Jarring, punishing. Being thrown is not the same as jumping, you're not ready. Pity that soldier, when I blink I see him lying somewhere, *must* be the ground then, wouldn't be the sky, would it. That poor old sod who cannot shift a limb, just glad it isn't me. It'd be the road he's lying on, blink twice, can see the white painted line, the indented stud of the cat's eye. There's a pain like a hammer in that man and it's pounding and squeezing him right down to mush, feel sorry for the old bugger I do, specially now seeing a bit've blood seeping out from him, running down into his neck it is, the pain in him, like a knife through the belly. Is he dying, that man, is that what it is? Course it's not a road, it's a battlefield really, that's how a battlefield looks after its been blitzed, chunks of bodies thrown about and the noise of screaming. I just imagined the white lines.

All the screeching and booming and scrunch of metal, that's stopped, there are softer noises, blurred and run together like words in a foreign language. Maybe it's the enemy come to kill the soldier, finish him off for good. But if I blink three times I see that there are faces, they are leaning over me. I try to point across to those sharp-angled hedges, try telling them they've made a mistake, that *I'm* not the one. Blink four times I see their lips move. I was very cold, my body was kind of juddering, but it's alright now, I think they've put something on top of me. A blanket. I'm gonna close me eyes for a bit and then when I open 'em again, if I'm still seeing the faces I'll know they are for real. I'm back on the road now, the soldier's in No Man's Land, other side of the hedge.

Course ya know, Elva with your black eyes all a dance, couldn't refuse you anything, not a thing, think of Christmas and the real-pearl pendant that you wanted . . .

'Hello.'

'Hello, to you,' says James. Opens his eyes, sees these two young girls standing just there over him, looking frightened, shivering a bit, it's cold November on top of the scare.

'They've called the ambulance, it won't be long,' the same girl says, all kind, kind eyes hers, she's kneeling down towards him. The other girl gives out a cry or makes some weird noise, says something he can't work out.

'No need for that,' he tells her. 'There's no need. It might look bad, but looks worse than it is, ya know. I'm not in pain or anything.' Those two girls both looking at him very kind, both still shivery, because of the fear or the cold. 'No, it's alright, but what's your names?' He's leaning up a bit now, on the wad of a rug or a cushion that's been put under his head.

'Sharon and Claire.'

'And how old are you, you girls?'

'Seventeen,' they say.

'Well listen now, Sharon and Claire, I'm very pleased to meet you. I shall have to go in the ambulance, but I don't need to. Could get up in a minute or two, bit of a shock of course, but I'll be alright in a minute. You girls got mobiles? No? Me neither. But if you could just take down this phone number then, if you wouldn't mind, if you've got a pen and a scrap of paper. Could you call my wife and let her know I'll have to go off in the ambulance, but only 'cause it's the expected thing. I'll be home in the morning right as rain. Got a pen?'

'Yeah,' Sharon, scared still, is writing the number down as he calls it out.

'Got it?'

'Yeah.'

'Tell her you talked to me and I'm alright. Alright?'

'Which one of you's Sharon?'

'Me.'

'So, then *you're* Claire.'

'Yeah.'

'So, don't you forget, you girls, Sharon and Claire. I don't want her worrying. Tell her she doesn't have to worry. Right.'

'The ambulance will be here in a minute,' say Sharon and Claire, and 'Yes, we promise to call her, but what's her name?'

'Little Elva. Well, ya know, *Elva* it is, but that's what I always call her. And there's one other thing you could do. Could you roll me a cigarette. The baccy's in my pocket.' Sharon finds the tin, Claire does the rollie with quaking hands. 'Now has either of you kind girls got a light?'

A light's worth more than a chest of gold would be.

He thinks of himself at home, at the in-laws', remembers Christmas, the rumpus and rows, Elva and her brother and her Mum having a go at one

LITTLE ELVA

another in Anglo-Italian improvisations, which can be hard to follow, then Elva's Dad getting in the fray, in Anglo-Italo-Catalan. James understands not a word, probably nobody else does. 'It's like bloody United Nations,' Mavis, the brother's wife from Bolton, says. And lying there on the road, he chuckles, seeing himself somehow got to the centre, shushing them down, holding the audience with his fluttering and blinking eyes, his mouth movements, his stylised hesitations, his stutter and mutter with which he keeps them waiting till it's time to tell, keeps 'em hanging on in until the punchline. He, holding them there, keeping the rumpus at bay, bringing on laughter with his pauses and his winks and the creased eye corners of his smile. *The timing he has, it's a bloody miracle.* And Little Elva, her eyes shining blackly for him, just for him as he takes the floor with this quiet charisma they say he has, so that unbelievably he is listened to, he holds the moment.

Now it's a different moment, he's lost the focus, is just there at the edge now hanging on, lying on the road, the turn of his feet at an awkward angle, looking uncomfortable but not *seeming* to hurt. There's his motorbike fallen sideways by the verge, near enough for him to just see the shine of torn off metal in a jagged heap. Sad sight, yes, but *he's* alright, that's the main thing, main thing isn't it, he himself is gonna be just fine. Better have a rest here for a little while, then go off in the ambulance, be on the safe side, though there's really no need. Sees Sharon and Claire and there's one or two more faces now in the shadows just behind 'em. *Is there anything he wants, anything that can be done?* Distant swush of voices in the dark. *A light, has anybody got a light?*

He'll be away from here quite soon, pity that poor soldier, pity the purple and scream of his pain, the gurgle of blood in him, the way he'll end up right there where he is, nowhere else to go to, nothing else now possible, done for, he's done. Dog with the eyes as big as saucers, dog with the eyes as big as soup plates, dog with the eyes as big as millwheels. What can we do for you, Master? as he hears the match strike, good girls that Sharon and Claire, smells the bit of sulphur, sees the flare. *Tell Little Elva everything's alright.*

THE DEUS EX MACHINA BIRD

O<small>N A HOT NIGHT IN JUNE</small>, Penny dances, starting off slowly, ending in a sizzle and shake, her two arms pressed forward from the shoulder, first one then the other, then both together. A sizzle-wriggle shake. Not bad for a woman of sixty-five, but you wouldn't know that and she won't have it stated, because she says, 'of the society we live in'. She's in a thin white halter top with tinny medallions sewn all over it, her flat-chestedness appearing to advantage, the nipples prominent. Twining one arm forward in a curling motion, then the other, then the two, the medallions coming into their own with a clanging, jangling clash. And when the arms are right there, pushed forward, elbows down, hands palm up, and the shoulders are lowered back, is when she starts the circle and swoop of the hips, bending her legs at the knee, giving that final pelvic thrust. The sweat on her is like a sheen. She's smooth and sweat-running and you imagine this heady oil, imagine her body plastered in it, rubbed to high finish. It will smell of patchouli or jasmine or honeysuckle rose.

It's now that the music takes a faster turn. Suddenly there's this speed to it, this vigour, a heat that spurts and meets the night with equal force. And Penny, she's right there with the excess of the moment, kindled by it, revelling, throwing her arms and her legs out wide, pushing her lithe and leathery torso forward towards the corner of the room. Then she's spinning round on her heels, repeating the giving gesture with extra emphasis to the room's centre, and to something else; to someone. From her slick bleached boys-look of a hairdo, to the sinew

THE DEUS EX MACHINA BIRD

in her arms, to the thrust out hips, there's this fired up intensity. She can't stop now, must go on to the climax of her act, and it's not far off. Not far now, she can feel it sliding up. And she leaps a little way to the left and then to the right, each time shaking her body so the medallions clink. And her head's nodding. Forwards and then back, once, twice, more times than you can count and getting faster, so that in the end it seems like one circular motion. Pips of sweat dart from the spiky ends of her hair, her ornate necklace bounces against her jutting neck bone. And see her face. It's held back at an unreal angle, a look of ecstasy, of parched and blighted somewhere-elseness—she's taken off. Now, it's the crescendo, her body is total shake and shimmer, so fast you can't see it happening, you can't see anything but blur. You hear nothing but the susurrating tin. Follow the direction her face is held, you'll become aware of a balcony with empty seats. Three rows back a man is standing with a furtive, crease-eyed stare, seeing nothing but the dancer; looking down from half hidden eyes which mirror the blind ferocity of her dance.

Amazingly, it's just this game with them, passion is already dead in her, had never been born in him—although this little simulacrum does have a real pleasure for them, making them feel as if they *are* alive, as if they too are a part of things and life isn't just a hopeless case. And the *form* will do, this is an attitude they share, in fact the form is the only thing, it's what they have respect for, it's what is held over the mush and dirtiness of the real, the squelch and reek of it. The form is a skin, concealing all. Penny and Derek see eye-to-eye in the matter of denial and each of them would completely resent an encounter with the world of feeling. That's why Penny can dance for Derek, there's no threat in it for either of them, no possibility of any repercussion.

No one else is dancing, most people are out by the river, sitting with drinks at the rows of tin-silver tables and the few in the room besides Penny are just talking in little groups, laughter spiralling out from time to time, at the telling of jokes or the recounting of funny incidents, the usual thing. The room is large, cream coloured, with the feel of an auditorium about it. They do live shows here, and pantomimes. Rapunzel is their big thing—the balcony makes it a must. When the music comes to an end, Penny stops dancing with a flourish, glances to the balcony. Derek's no longer there and she bows to empty space.

Out on the terrace Ralph and Alice sit in an irritated silence. Ralph can be very acerbic when crossed, Alice is good at crossing. If Ralph was a smoker he'd be chain smoking, as it is he's biting at a little piece of tough skin on the side of his thumb, his task being to make the surface smooth again. Alice looks up at an overhanging tree and then out at the river, annoyingly serene. But you never know when she'll turn that's the thing, *he* never knows. Another thing he doesn't know is what would be worse. After as careful thinking as he can muster when his head is pounding with so much irritation, he decides that the serenity is not as bad as the turning would be, thus he quietens, picks up his glass composedly so that no wine splashes from it, drinks. But an important thing Ralph doesn't know, something that hasn't even occurred to him, is that this quietly blissful look of Alice's is the precursor to some kind of nastiness which could range from the making of a remark he'll hate down to a sneer pointedly aimed. It takes very little to rile him, and despite his carefully contrived manner of rational politeness, where women are concerned he's a simple tyrant expecting that they'll always follow where he chooses to lead. He never listens to their opinions and the only jokes he can tolerate from them are ones which conspire at their own self abasement. At these he will laugh with a dry doglike howl in his throat, his mouth making extraordinary contortions. No such joke is forthcoming; the laugh does not happen.

'Why will you go back to Brussels, seeing as you don't like being there?' Alice has turned to face Ralph, looks right at him with her eyes of clearest blue, eyes which are not in the mood for evasion. Behind the question the inference that it's because of Penny, that Penny has undue influence on his choices, on everything he decides to do, an idea which makes Ralph burn with fury, as Alice sees. So she follows up the words with a smirk placed at the level of Ralph's throat—his *eyes* are held away from her.

Ralph's face is red, nearly matching his hair in depth of colour by the time Penny and Derek come up to the table, and Alice looks as though she's been bitten—there's a kind of indented double line in her cheek like an *equals* sign, which *could* have been made by a set of teeth, and it's deepening by the second. There's an atmosphere with a capital A, a situation which is right up Penny's street. Penny can sniff trouble at a surprising distance, she detected it here when she and Derek were only half way across the floor just by seeing the set angle of Ralph's shoulder and the tight way he was clenching his glass. She perches on the nearest chair paying no attention to Alice. Alice is on her way out. Knowing this makes Penny gracious. She gives the moment her best. Derek too, *knows* things, he has his intuitions in the matter of stray emotions, takes in quickly that Alice is out there, unconnected, bruised in some indefinable way, looking for support.

'Well, hello,' Penny comes out with gushingly, her lips all smile, which Alice her former protégée does her best to edit right out of her consciousness. Alice scowls, which makes Penny's smile broaden to face-splitting proportions. Alice wishes it *would* split. She herself is fluttery, all nerves, but it's okay because here's Derek, and Derek has all kinds of signs flashing across his features, one of which is: *Alice, I think you're gorgeous.* He's looking at her under his eyelids in that way he has which Alice finds sexy, and just at this moment finds *incredibly* sexy, and he follows up the look with a private small smile which she returns. Nevertheless she perceives very clearly the look of gratitude on Ralph's face as Penny joins them fussily at the table, and it makes her mad.

'And the theatre manager said it couldn't be done that way and told us we'd have to go back for the new key,' Penny says to the others matter of factly on arrival momentarily stunning them with lack of comprehension, so that they're silent and self questioning. In those crucial few minutes she takes control. Derek, a seasoned games player is the first to recover and he makes a rapid attempt to ignore Penny altogether, which is okay by her anyway, because he is already doing what she'd brought him here to do. Ralph on the other hand gets sucked in, saying sarcastically to Penny, 'What key?' for he's entirely incapable of passing over the smallest opportunity for pointing out that any woman is an irrational moron.

'The key to the cupboard!' Penny says, shaking her head at him as though in disbelief at his lack of concentration. And the two of them are immediately hunting round for allies, Ralph seriously compromising himself by making sudden moist eyed overtures to Alice. Derek, in a state of fierce secret rivalry with Ralph at once falls in with Penny, nodding as though he takes her meaning, and Alice, to be on the side of Derek at this moment rather than Ralph, does likewise, which leaves Ralph out in the cold. This is always the way and it makes him fear and loathe Penny in a violent burst.

'What key?' he repeats snappishly, unwilling to concede. It's misjudged. The other three are already chatting about the swiftness of the current in the river below the terrace and he is ignored. The reminder of his essential isolation hits home as Penny intended that it would.

'So, I'm planning a little going away party,' Penny says, switching to the subject of Ralph's imminent return to Brussels. She's reinforcing the idea of how much Ralph needs her, how lost he'd really be if ever she turned her back on him.

'Are you going somewhere?' Ralph asks her in that insulting tone he reserves especially for talking to Penny.

'No,' she says right back, overriding him. '*You* are.'

Penny's taken the moment but then, unpredictably Alice cuts in with, 'Where would any of us be without you, Penny. You know where we're all going better than we do ourselves.' Her smile is radiant, it draws Ralph and Derek to her. The three of them seem welded together suddenly and Penny's the one out in the cold. A little triumph. There's a silence — what's to say. Then Penny gives a shriek making the others uneasy. What's she come up with now?

'Look!'

THE DEUS EX MACHINA BIRD

They glance round helplessly, trying not to make it obvious they're at a loss then see Penny stretch sideways and scoop up a small feathery thing.

'Oh a young bird,' says Alice. 'It must have fallen out of that tree. It's dead, poor baby. Or it soon will be.'

'They die of shock, don't they,' Ralph announces, his voice complacent.

Penny ignores them and wraps the bird in a table napkin before laying it tenderly in a pocket of her bag. So that, in spite of everything, she steals the show.

Penny at home with all the lights on because she can't bear the thought of death. She has the radio turned up, the TV blasting, and she keeps on checking herself in the many mirrors on the walls of her flat, because silence and invisibility are like twin gateways to annihilation. When she's on her own there's really little activity happening with her, apart from the shift and twitch of fear and this incessant restless meandering through all the rooms, particularly the bathroom because the mirror there is the most flattering to her appearance. And she has the phone with her at all times of course. Dana has just split up with John, she's been on the phone to Penny on and off all evening. *No, she's not suicidal, but yes, she might come over. It's the shock.* No shock to Penny though, she'd seen it coming, she usually does.

Then Ralph. *His* flat has all the lights *off* because he can't bear to see the state of things. *Yes, Penny will come round to Lancaster Gate tomorrow. She'll help him to sort it out.* Penny smirks into her phone, glances through into the bedroom at the little light feathered bird which she's placed by the window on a coat hanger suspended from the top of the roller blind. She's tied the bird to the strut so it won't fall off. No way is that bird dead or even close to death. Predictably, Ralph's depressed—things aren't working out with Alice. Well, Penny could have told him that. *In fact, at the moment he and Alice aren't really speaking.* Penny purses her lips to herself in the bathroom mirror, reaches for her vermillion lipstick from the cosmetics shelf, unfurls the lid one handed, applies it in a thick voluptuous line.

Baker Street, one-thirty. Alice is already waiting, Penny sees that her eyes are red but unrelenting. *Principles, that's what it is.* Alice has principles, well so be it, principles will be Alice's downfall. The two women walk together towards Regent's Park, Penny registering every admiring glance from men that Alice receives en route. And it's true that Alice, who is all aglow with high feeling, has a kind of fiery burnished look.

If Ralph must insist on going to Brussels for these three months then he must announce their engagement before he goes. This is Alice's pronouncement, and she snaps her mouth over the end of the sentence to emphasise it's her final word. Penny is deeply sympathetic, she *does* see Alice's point of view, and she also knows perfectly well that on top of everything else is Alice's anxiety about 'the biological clock'. She's thirty-seven, or is it eight? Mmm. They haven't discussed this aspect of the situation, but still Penny is quite aware that it's paramount. 'Or I won't know *what* to think.' Alice bites back the tremor just starting on her lip.

Penny is also aware that Alice doesn't trust her, but has needed to see her anyway as the most likely way of reaching Ralph. She won't ask of course, but she *does* want Penny to intercede, all the same. After all, it was Penny who introduced them, surely this means Penny must have *some* interest in seeing them both happy, in bringing things together. Penny pieces together all the bits of reasoning that Alice is likely to be going through, ending with the self guilt at the idea Penny is against her. *And why should Penny be against her, after all it's not as if there could be any sense of rivalry, not at her age.* Alice is very unimaginative in her outlook. It makes Penny laugh. They're sitting right now on a bench in the Inner Circle, the smell of roses wafting across to them. It's gloriously warm. Penny pats the hand of her friend, says, 'Why not carry on having the relationship without worrying about having the acknowledgement?'

'What, and let *him* determine everything?'

THE DEUS EX MACHINA BIRD

Penny smiles. She knew that Alice wouldn't buy this one, that things have already gone too far for her rather forthright character, as it is. But she likes to keep to the outward letter of things, and nobody can accuse her now of not giving Alice the benefit of her advice.

'Let me treat you to lunch,' she says with satisfaction. 'The time's getting on. And, er, Alice, I'll try and see what I can do. Maybe he'll listen to reason, though I can't make any promises, he *is* stubborn, as you know.'

'Thank you,' Alice mumbles, blushing because of the ignominy of being here and getting comfort from hearing such words from Penny whom she has ceased to like.

Sitting with Derek later that day in Soho, outside the Bar Italia, Penny lets herself fall into the half-flirting, half-scolding mode that always seems to happen to her when she's with him. He's looking cool in his ice blue satinised shirt, his almost blonde hair catching all the gold of the light. When Ralph was in the process of dumping Penny two years ago for a younger woman, she'd brought Derek in on the scene as an experiment with the mechanics of control. She just wanted to see if she couldn't cause a little upheaval. Derek had a dual role to play, first as the admirer, maybe even the lover, of Penny herself (till she'd twigged he was incapable), and secondly as the seducer of Lorna, Ralph's new woman. Derek's impotence was a bonus, if anything. He was safe, he wouldn't ever desert her for one of the younger women, she could preserve the form of their affair. She'd even stepped up on the flirtation. But the double nature of Derek's role *did* give Penny a bit of disquiet because it was like sanctioning the structure of her own betrayal. Nevertheless she bore it, thinking of the whole thing as a kind of play, which in fact it was. It had all ended up as a bit of a tangle, and whatever else was true, the departure of Lorna was certainly brought about by the unsavoury and seedy atmosphere of the dynamic the latter stages of which were pure hysteria. Scandalous gossip and accusations went flying around on a daily basis. The upshot of all of that was that Penny, for whom the experiment had been an unqualified success, now held on to *both* men by continually reproducing the original triangle with stand-ins for Lorna. Alice had come into the picture in the first place in this role, and it was now high time, in Penny's opinion, for Derek to finish her off.

'She's so wild,' Penny says of Alice, exaggerating hugely to inflame him, she knows what *will*. The very idea of wildness, a quality he can't imagine but would like to own, to strut out with, to tame, to not be frightened of. It's the challenge of it that will get to him. She sips her coffee, waits, sees that his eyes have gone glazed. He's hiding from her. Good, that means something.

'So, the *party*,' she says at once, making sure that the connection between his desire and the opportunity for fulfilment won't be lost on him. Derek is acting completely casual, but he's clocked the information, Penny knows it. She's confident now, the process has happened so many times. 'Anyway, Alice is very lovely, isn't she,' Penny says carefully, feeling a hurtful twinge of jealousy on hearing the words out loud. Derek says nothing. Most probably he's already started rehearsing the seduction of Alice, Penny thinks. He has that far off dreamy look. She's satisfied, with just a streak of anger at his disloyalty, but then he's a desperate case, emotionally incapable of any sort of real relationship, and so what, she asks herself, can she expect?

At The Swan on the Bayswater Road, Ralph leans against the bar moodily, and Penny can hardly get a word out of him. They're just around the corner from his flat, which is where they're headed so that Penny can have the pleasure of preparing his supper, but still, she doesn't mind this, it's just another of the ways she keeps control. It's a sultry late evening with a threat of rain in the sky. The rain doesn't materialise, but there's a kind of pent-up heaviness.

Ralph's special insulting way of speaking to Penny doesn't happen when they're in private, it's only when they're in company with younger women, to whom he's trying hard to demonstrate his complete separateness from Penny, plus his availability. Penny, playing a game based on her knowledge that Ralph loves to go completely against any advice she ever gives him, is bombarding him with her conviction he should give things with Alice another go. She points out to him that Alice is tempestuous and doesn't really mean what she says, this to make him aware that Alice is trouble and won't be easy to handle, all of which will make Ralph more wary than he already is. Ralph is almost too easy, he isn't even what Penny would consider a challenge, but then it isn't a challenge she's after, it's simply to maintain her power base. Bitterness at the way he dumped her always supplies the drive. If she was twenty years younger he'd have married her, and it wasn't even as if he wanted children. But it was the age thing that stopped him and she knows that secretly he's ashamed of having been with a woman so many years his senior. She no longer feels resentment in a clear cut way, but it's there somewhere all the same, breaking out in bursts of glee when his so-called relationships inevitably crash. She looks objectively at his thinning light rust hair and his pinkish neck with its tendency to freckle. This now seems infinitely less boyish that it did five years ago on account of the roll of fat—a recent neck development in tune with the general thickening of his body. *She* is in better shape that *he* is, no question of it. They finish their beers and leave quite soon after so that Penny will have plenty of time to make his seafood platter just the way he likes to have it.

On a hot night in July, Penny has her party. Her flat in Norfolk Square is on the ground floor and the doors to the garden are open, trellis and bushes all festooned with lantern lights supplied by Derek's theatrical design company. In the garden it's surprisingly quiet for a Saturday night, with just the sound of distant traffic from the Edgware Road. Penny always does things festively. Three tables stand out on the lawn decked with flowers, bowls of fruit, and ice buckets for the white wine. To keep the wine cool, fresh cold ice is added on a frequent basis by

GOD OF THE PIGEONS

David, a new friend of Penny's who's started hanging out with her on account of all her young women acquaintances. He won't do as an understudy for Derek though, Penny divined instantly, he doesn't possess the charm. But he's okay to have around. Penny likes to have people around, to make up the numbers, fill up the empty space and give her the feeling something is happening. Anyway, she must always be the nucleus, and how could she *be* a nucleus without accretions? But most of all, these people are the equivalent of the lights she has to keep on in her flat at night so that she won't have to think of any of the bad things. And this David is polite and willing to take orders, in the hope. *As long as he doesn't hold his breath*. This thought is Penny's idea of a joke. Cutting a decorative but inedible looking cake into slices, which she arranges stylishly on a plate, she chuckles.

Ralph has only just arrived and he's sitting stonily by the table in the sitting room, to Penny's practised eye clearly on the look out for Alice, though pathetically pretending not to be. He chews impatiently at a couple of celery sticks, getting strands stuck in the gaps between his teeth then trying to extrapolate them with an angry hand, glaring at Penny as though she'd devised this means of bringing about his humiliation.

'Only Ralph could be so gauche,' she muses, acting as though she hasn't seen him. The celery strands stretch and ping like rubber bands. Penny clucks her tongue. But his ineptitude and unattractive ways are as valuable to Penny as Derek's sexual problems, the glue which binds him to her. She leaves him to his misery, going to open the door to more people, and when she returns there *is* Alice, and she and Ralph are already having one of those very heated discussions they're so good at. Penny gives Alice a vivacious wave and edges a bit closer in order to hear them.

'Why say *interstices* when you can say *cracks*?' Ralph has his biting voice, one that even Penny can't bear the sound of. There's a bit of a silence, perhaps Alice will have capitulated, but no, Penny hears her voice ring out. 'Interstices sound as if you have to crawl into them, wriggle sideways, you know, adapt yourself a bit, make an effort. Cracks are cracks.' Her voice is slightly hysterical, Penny thinks, and it's no wonder, Ralph *can* be a trial. And right at this moment when Ralph's face has gone crimson with intense annoyance along comes Derek right on cue, saying, 'What was that about *wriggling*?' Penny has to turn away.

No, Ralph is *not* having a good party. Alice has disappeared, *God only knows where Alice is*. He looks at Penny with reproach each time he catches sight of her.

'Let's go into the garden,' she says at last, looking at her watch. It's about eleven-thirty, things are settling down.

What they see when they get there, both of them at once, and without any possibility of avoidance is Alice in the arms of Derek in a stagy, overblown embrace. Alice, romantic fool that she is, is lost to the world, but everything about Derek is posturing and insincere, world aware. This is Penny's happy observation anyway. Remaining still for a second or two to be sure Ralph takes in the little *tableau vivant* they're being treated to, Penny then guides him back in the direction of the house. She is suave, sphinx-like, yawning with light and insouciant affectation. She pats at her mouth, concealing mixed emotions. Hatred for Alice the rival, pity for Alice the loser and the dupe. Pity for herself, hatred for Ralph, perhaps love, or if not love as such, at least the semblance of a residue. She re-lives the taste of her own past rejection, the rank-blood flavour of it. Horrific, but it lasts only a second, the cut-out is almost immediate. Alice is wiped away forever and Penny has a moment of true serenity. Everything's clean now, all that's dirty has come out in the wash.

'Oh, Dana,' she says composedly when they reach the hall, to a slim pale looking woman of about thirty-three, not what you'd call beautiful by a long shot, but with masses of blonde hair. Yes, Penny feels serene, she's moving on, she experiences a sense of personal release. On the tail of these positive emotions a twinge of fresh jealousy kicks in however, because what she's moving onto is only more of the same. Dana, who now has *her* role to play in Penny's tragic farce.

GOD OF THE PIGEONS

All the games must go on, they have to go on. The form must be preserved, for what else is there that can hide the real so well? The noise, the people, the lights. Penny is unable to do without them. Dana, like the other female leads before her, will always be part-rival, part-representation of Penny herself, on both counts for Dana personally, it's a no-win situation.

'Oh, Dana,' Penny says again, with the faint anxiety of a procuress, wanting things to go well, wanting things to go *spectacularly* well, but starting at once on the familiar path of grief and secret bitterness, 'You really must meet Ralph. Ralph, this is Dana. Dana and I are thinking of taking a little holiday in Belgium. Maybe we could look you up.'

Inside the flat, on the window ledge in Penny's bedroom, the puffball bird on his coat hanger sways stiff and silent, his bright eyes fixed. Penny will leave him out for a while to have a full look at him, then put him away again in the box where he lives until she feels the need to bring him out of it. She's had him for a year or two now. She'd bought him once at a nature park gift shop to be trotted out as and when. She's fond of him, though it's not what you'd call a sentimental fondness, more a recognition of the usefulness of having props to hand to help her keep a scene going or whatever. She's also got a spider, a lizard and a plastic rose. Any of these items can be thrown down unnoticed under a table or somewhere when the moment seems to call for it. Because no matter what's true and what isn't true—and in Penny's way of looking at things, who gives a toss really which is which—the show must always go on. Penny looks up at her bedroom window, sees Puffball's rocky shadow through the glass. She waves.

CAN I BE DANDINI?

There's that yellow girl. So dry and runny, I can't help thinking of an egg. She sits wishy-washy at the end of the wall, face powdery as eggshell, eyes with this watery look. Right now a tooth is resting against her lower lip, she's dreaming, I suppose. I don't like her much, she's not that friendly. Her name is Celia. In class she sits next to the girl with sticky-out eyes who keeps white mice and picks bogies from her nose which she wipes on the side of the desk. Val. She isn't friendly either. It's playtime, the early home-to-dinners are just getting back. That Val has come in the gate and is skipping across the playground. She'll come over to the wall. That's where the two of them always perch themselves. I haven't sat here before, I'm just trying it out today to see what it feels like. Val is pale and freckly. Weetabix and milk. Val always stares at me and talks to Celia behind her hand and then the two of them get the giggles. They'll giggle all through class usually and other kids have to keep on saying *Shhhh*. If you say *Shhhh* a lot they'll finally shut up though Val will keep on with the staring. Celia draws chicks with her felt tips. Now and then she'll do a few split open eggshells to show you where the chicks have come from, but what she likes best is just doing these rows and rows of chicks. I move up and let Val in and she and Celia start giggling right away. I knew it would be awful on this wall. I'll sit here till the bell and then that's it. I'm not coming back tomorrow.

'D'you like dancing?' Val suddenly asks me, pointing out her toes.

'Yes,' I say.

'D'you go dancing, then?'

I know they both know I go dancing 'cause they've seen me coming out of the church annex with my shoe bag, so I keep quiet.

GOD OF THE PIGEONS

'Yes, she does,' Celia tells Val when I don't answer, and I don't like that sarky voice she's putting on. Now she's pointing out her toes the same as Val.

'Where does she go?' Val asks Celia.

'Who, the cat's mother?' I say. They ignore me and start swaying slowly in time, stretching out their legs as far as they can and pointing their toes close together. The giggling's got really loud now. I'm never sitting on this horrible wall again, it's a lot nicer on the seat by the girls' toilets or next to the flowerbed by the gate.

'So do we,' Celia says.

'Yeah,' goes Val. 'We go dancing.'

'Where d'you go,' I can't help asking 'em.

'It's fantastic,' Celia tells me, swinging her yellowy hair.

'Where is it?'

'Over our way.'

They live on the other side of town to me, I've never been there. I wish I could see the fantastic dance place. Where I go dancing is just this church annex with a stone floor. It's a bit dusty, makes me sneeze.

'What's it like?' I ask.

'It's a white room with all mirrors round, and a marble floor,' Celia says.

'Yeah,' goes Val.

'Wow,' I say. 'Where I go is dusty and the floor's rough.'

They both make a scrunched-up face at me, then up come the hands. Sound of whispering. They're staring through fingers at me. Next minute they jump up from the wall and whirl across the playground with their arms flying out.

'We're butterflies with wings,' Val calls to me.

'We're flying angels.'

I come back to the wall the next day, I want to hear more about where they go dancing. I keep on trying to picture that white room.

'The mirrors have got gold frames,' Celia tells me. 'With cherubs.'

CAN I BE DANDINI?

'Cherubs?'

'Yeah, in the gold. The walls are covered in the cherub mirrors and the ceiling's pale blue with silver stars.'

'We're gonna be real ballerinas when we leave school,' says Val.

They get off the wall and poise themselves at the edge of the playground. Then they start to spin. Celia looks slightly gold in the sunrays, and Val seems silver, sequinned. I wish I could be like them.

It's Tuesday. I sat on the wall all last week and yesterday. They have gorgeous ballet dresses at the dance school. Celia's is white gauze with loads of sparkles that shimmer all the colours of the rainbow when she dances. And there's hundreds of dresses they can choose from. The one I like the sound of best has got a blue velvet top. I wonder if it would fit me. Oh, and Celia and Val have pink satin ballet shoes. Mine are only red leather with an elastic to hold them on. Theirs have matching pink satin ribbons that criss cross over their ankles. Celia says they have points. The three of us practise dancing on points by squeezing our big toes up inside our sandals. We have to go fast so we won't topple. It's great. We get a quarter way across the playground before we collapse.

There's just one thing I want to know. Can I go to Celia's ballet school? When I asked 'em they said it was very difficult to get in, but I'd do anything. Val told me there was a waiting list. And there's something else bothering me. Would I be good enough? I just don't know. Oh, but I do so want to go. If they'd tell me where it is maybe I could get my Mum to take me.

Me—*So where is it?*

Celia—*Where's what?*

Me—*You know, the ballet school.*

Celia—*It's near us.*

Val—*Outside it's got white pillars.*

Celia—*And inside.*

Val—*It's gonna be on TV.*

Me—*When?*

GOD OF THE PIGEONS

Celia—*At Christmas.*
Val—*A pantomime.*
Me again—*Oh, can I come and watch it?*
Celia and Val together—*Nobody's allowed at the rehearsals.*

I start asking them if they think I'd be able to get in the ballet school soon, but half way through the question the two of them have gone off on their points, linking arms, Val saying they were being Cinderella and Prince Charming.

'Can I be Dandini?' I call out after them, but they can't hear me 'cause they've had to go fast, to stop from toppling over.

When I get home I tell my Mum I don't want to go to my old ballet school any more, I want to go to Celia's. She doesn't seem to listen.

'Please let me go,' I say six times.

Mum makes a sighing noise. 'Where is it?'

'I don't know,' I have to tell her.

'Well, why don't you find out?' is what she says.

Blue butterfly wings on the flying Princess Celia, the golden ballerina. Red Velvet butterfly wings fluttering on the shoulders of Princess Val, the silver dancer. They land together in the bright-white ballroom, rest their hands on the bar of pink pearl. They stretch out their legs from skirts of foamy net, glimmering like stars. The ballet teacher in a black lycra leotard, her hair pulled up into a knot on her head, points towards them. Her perfect red lips are smiling. She twirls on the spot to the sound of piano music, sunshine pours in through crystal windows. It's a magic scene. And look, here's another little butterfly gliding across the marble floor. She has wings of vivid green with real emerald borders and a bronze metallic skirt. Oh wow . . . it's me!

'How much is it to join?' I hope my Mum can afford it, I hope it's not too dear. 'So is it very near to yours?' I ask them. 'Can you walk there?' 'Do you have to get the bus?'

CAN I BE DANDINI?

We're sitting on the wall, it's dinner time. Maybe they're not going to tell me.

Their eyes are misty, swim with laughter, they do not speak.

'Mum,' I ask when I get home. 'Will *you* ask 'em if I can go?·I can't find out where it is, they won't tell me. Please ask them, Mum.'

My Mum sighs.

It feels funny, Mum coming into the playground. Kids stare as she walks with me across to the wall. It all seems to have gone very quiet.

In the distance I see the long low wall and the two crouching bodies of Val and Celia. 'That's them,' I say to Mum when we're a bit closer up.

I stand back and she goes over. I don't want to hear what she says to 'em, I feel too embarrassed.

She leans down, hand on hip, her black coat flap flapping in the wind making her look like a bird. She looks like a rook or a raven with sleek shiny feathers. I imagine a sharp bird beak. I see Val through the triangle Mum's arm makes. A face which is white, not silver, with goggly eyes red around the rim and mouse-like which follow each slight movement of Mum's face. Val's lips, pale and fallen apart seem to quiver to the rhythm of every word. I edge to the left and see Celia's bare and runny eyes, slits in her blind eggshell face, held upwards as though expecting to be cracked.

Oh please, I want all this to stop. I want Mum to go away. I don't like her leaning down to 'em like that and talking on and on. Mum's voice is loud and booming, Val and Celia shiver on the wall. And it's all my fault. It's giving me a pain, I think I'm going to be sick. *Ow*, it hurts. They look like feeble jelly creatures. Celia grinds her teeth—sound of breaking eggshell. Then her thin cracked voice comes out jerkily, shuddering in little broken words I can't quite hear.

Stop it, I say inside myself. I'm going to cry.

Grey wall, grey afternoon sky. Gold and silver gone to grey. Grey world, grey everything. My heart's grey too, wrung out like a dirty dishcloth. My eyes are full of dishwater. I close them, feel the dishwater trickle down my cheeks. And I hear Mum's voice driving on and on, a scolding sound. I want to disappear, I want to be in a different place.

At last it's over, Mum has straightened up and moved away from the wall. She's smoothing back the collar of her coat and going. Striding along towards the school gates. I trail along behind her, seeing a quick blur of two grey figures still seated on the wall, as I turn my head. I don't look at them again.

It's the same going back across the playground as it was coming over. Talk fades to patches of silence around us as we pass, it's so horrible. I still have the pain, and I feel a fool. I feel such a fool.

We're at the gates and Mum pauses to get her breath. I catch her up and wait, as she expects me to, scraping at the ground with the toe of my shoe.

'There is no dance school,' she says crossly. 'I really wish you wouldn't waste my time like this.'

I nod, I'd understood everything as soon as Mum had come up to the wall. There wasn't any beautiful white ballroom after all. 'But why did they pretend there was one?' I ask Mum.

'Well,' she says. 'Why do you think?' Then she shakes her head, 'Going to a real dancing school costs money. They just dance at home, in the kitchen.'

I'm filled with shame, for them, for myself. I can't look at Mum.

'You might have known,' she says more quietly.

I turn and run back into the playground. I know what Mum means now. She means because they're poor. I don't want to hear that. I want them to be rich and happy in that white and silver world. I don't want to hear about Val's bobbly cardigan and Celia's worn-thin school skirt. And other things. I don't want to hear about the two of them looking undernourished and being a bit grubby and not wearing socks inside their sandals. These are the sort of things Mum always talks about. I should never have brought her here, I see now you can't let a grown-up in on anything special without the spell being broken.

CAN I BE DANDINI?

The next day Celia and Val won't move up for me on the wall. They whisper together and look beyond me as if I'm not really there at all. In class Val picks her nose and holds a wet red and yellow bogie on the end of her finger, examining it. Celia starts a fresh row of chicks, doing all the tops of the heads together, and then all the beaks. Neither one of them speaks to me.

At dinnertime I'm going to stand in the porch next to the school kitchen with Susie, Paula, and Jenny Rice. Jenny says the dinner ladies sometimes give you lollies which run out because there are never enough to go round, and it's always first come first served. It's summer now, we play Fairies and Witches and Scissor-Paper-Stone, and the lollies melt quickly, making our fingers orange.

BEAUTY QUEENS

THREE BEAUTY QUEENS IN the bandstand: Candy, Dierdre and Shereen. Here they sit at the centre of everything, in hot summer sunshine. The bandstand is set in a wide marked-off green where events are to take place, like the children's annual fancy dress parade at three o'clock. The green is surrounded by looped ropes behind which is the crowd, or the audience, as the three of them like to say, and all the sideshows of the fete. It's just like being in a movie, Candy thinks. She pictures the opening credits running over the green, then the camera pans across to the bandstand. She's on close-up. She smiles. It's quarter to two, the three of them sit waiting for the photographer.

Candy has changed her name from Mandy, Dierdre's always been Dierdre. As for Shereen, she's forgotten who she is half the time, there'd be no point in increasing her confusion by casting doubts. Candy would prefer her name to begin with a K though because that sounds sharper. She wants to be sweet, but the special kind of sharp sweet that K has to it, high kicking into air, not gooey or salivary or round. She does her nails bright red with sparkle. This is sugary and sharp; favours eyes shadowed in silver, vamp lashes and brows. K things. Candy's mouth is voluptuous in a narrow-lipped way, very expressive. She pencils a fine line round her lips, emphasising their roomy angularity, does the centre in gloss, smiles a lot, 'Well, you have to,' is what she says.

Candy and Shereen have this way of defying the tendency of the world around them, only they do it differently. Dierdre's really had it with the Beauty Queen Scene, then there's part of her that wants to hang on to it forever, which makes her despondent because she knows you can't. But the force of realism is very strong in Dierdre, it's equally her strength and weakness. Candy and Shereen have their strengths and weaknesses in other ways. They're not really on a continuum with Dierdre in the middle, Candy at the sky end with her unpinnable butterfly wings, Shereen, opposite, sunk and getting lower, it's just that Dierdre is attracted by the idea of a seesaw and of being the central pivot where nothing nasty can happen. Because you are always the same fixed height from the ground you know where you are. It might make you bitter what you know, but that's the price you have to pay. She looks around her. Candy, up in the clouds where she always is, probably not being here at all, except as an after image, a photograph. Shereen, way down there, her eyes with a hooded look as though she doesn't want to see. Both smiling though, it's automatic, been doing it for quite a while, doing it charmingly and unthinkingly. Red lipstick, smiley lips, tools of the trade. Has to be a red which can be seen from a distance, subtlety's of no value, they're on show, they have to be seen to be happy. Dierdre too, on her make-believe seesaw, smiling out at audience, no trouble at all. Get the smile right and you'll be perceived as beautiful. Of course Dierdre and Candy will not be beautiful, not the way Shereen is naturally, but even so she has to have the red lips too because natural beauty isn't enough. They're acting the parts of Perfect Beauty. That's why Candy's here doing this, settling opinion in her white and silver swimsuit, not that she's a dog. But the three of them, it's what they're all up to, glitter and make believe. Except that Dierdre's coming to terms, the other two couldn't handle it. Now Dierdre thinks of a canoe. She's sitting in the middle, the only one with a paddle. The other two're up the Swanee but there's nothing you can say to them, they are what they are. Dierdre is experiencing the symmetry of her body, she feels good, twiddles the fingers of both hands, then her toes, sits straight on the velvet chair, not cross-legged, knees together, feet even, enjoying her composure. Shereen's thinking she won't go home tonight, she'll stay with Phil, put up with his incomprehensible laughter which seems to find her funny. If she disagrees with anything he's said, this laughter comes, subverting her objections in a lighthearted way. She thinks of smithereens, in her mind picks up the broken pieces of her hopes.

Beauty queens in the bandstand looking out at sunshine. In satin stretch swimsuits they sit on velvet chairs, Shereen between Candy and Dierdre, with her shiny blue sash, with flowers in a see-through wrapper tied with a ribbon, also blue: MISS MIDLANDS, QUEEN OF QUEENS. Sitting regally, far-off look to her, but she's in bits, really her life is in bits. Smiling from her throne across the recreation ground, in the Midlands heartlands, sunny Saturday, no wind. Winner, the queen of queens, a thought to hang onto, maybe it will draw her together, she can't go on like this. Tears gel and settle inside her head, not showing themselves. The bad inside her, the foul things, are what she lets out in secret, only smiles are for sharing. While Dierdre, paddling her invisible canoe, holds the other two at equal distances achieving balanced weight—she'll never topple, never go to highs or lows—and star struck Candy contemplates the glory of this perfect moment, kicking high into it, her smile genuine for this magic she'd like to keep forever. She's loving every minute, feeling unreal in a safe way, as though she's made of plastic and indestructible, an image on a screen, picture in a book, a hologram. A living moment, yes, but somehow inorganic, nothing frightening, so smoothly serene it's making her strong and capable, she can't be stopped. Miss Electro Zytek Cables, got her eye on eternity, that's for sure.

Candy, Dierdre and Shereen in their roped-off moment, glorious sun this day, sky's so blue. Bit of perfection to the look and feel of it, an air of excitement which they breathe right in. Even Dierdre postpones her knowledge of necessary changes which will remove her from this seat to the world of the commonplace, glossing over the six week pregnancy, her sickness, the agonies of the everyday. Just now she's charmed by the sun, she flings out her lustrous black hair, and it's no strain to smile, comes quite naturally to her lips. Wide green sweep of the recreation ground with stalls in an irregular line, little fun stalls with awnings, selling junk, and dolls and books and cakes, and there's a hotdog stand with oniony smoke going up in a gust, a barbecue with singeing sausage fat, hoopla and 'guess the number of peas in the jar' and tombola and the raffle table with the sherry bottles and cellophane-boxed fruit. The bandstand is at the centre of it all, making Dierdre happy, as though she's supporting all of the fete around them with her waving hand, and the fete likewise is counterbalancing, propping her up, will never let her fall. She's protected in this special moment, whatever seediness tomorrow might bring.

The mayor's passing, giving the girls a wink, they're still all smiles. Shereen with her special one, squeezing her tongue between her teeth so that it peeps out at the sides, little bit of spit on the lips, shoulders shrugged in, hiccough style. He's off in the sun and bluster, cockade of his hat flimsy in the wind, glint and glitter of his mayoral office chains. Givin 'em the eye, those girls. 'What's new?' he calls. They look out to the wide green space, the barriers, and there's the crowd, the crowd that makes the being here worthwhile. Dierdre adjusts the little coronet that's started slipping, she's feeling queasy. Oh please, no. Not now of all times, she's determined not to give way to it. She gulps in air, grips her side, and the coronet slips further. But she's having to hold her body tight in place, so never mind that, she can't let go of herself, it would spell disaster. The mayor turns and grins back at the three of them, grins as he makes his way across the green, hand to hat, it's getting more windy by the minute. Dierdre burps silently and tastes the taste of day-old cabbage, not that she's eaten any, just the thought of it makes her want to puke.

'Where's the damn photographers?' says Candy, voicing all their impatience at being kept waiting. 'We're s'posed to be the stars of this show, why aren't they here?' And now it's not sunny suddenly, the sky's a flabby wilting grey, old socks, unwashed underwear, a mildewed look, you could imagine it smelling as bad. Makes Dierdre feel ill, Shereen depressed, Candy disbelieving. Such a bright sunshiny sky turned into a day so dark the audience is scattering. Candy waves as though to draw the people back again. Must have them here, must. How can you be a Beauty Queen without them? Candy, Miss Electro Zytek Cables, holding fast to her belief in the sovereignty of this moment come rain or shine, even if it's rain. And it is, here come the first few splashes.

Shereen know's what's happening with her mum and dad. Things are going on that she's seen the signs of, her mum's vague giggling, as though it's too late for practical solutions and laughter is all that's possible, her dad's dissolute eye, disowning trouble, yet by just looking the way he does, a sure sign it's coming thick and fast. She's seen it all before, knows they're getting ready to do a flit, she can sense it's close. She bites her lip which spoils her image a bit, but it's gone so dark and windy nobody can really see. Then she thinks of her very secret place, the little cut where she'd let out all the bad, had screamed in part-pain, part-pleasure at the time of the cutting, had regretted nothing since. A private opening through which her grief had gushed. *Ow.*
    Friends coming round, having to say, 'Sit with your legs together because of my dad.' To Dell, to her best friend Dell, 'You know, he'll try, he'll try to look up your skirt, make sure your skirt's around you, no gaps.' Her voice had shaken when she'd first forced herself to say those words. Shereen thinks of the time her dad had touched her in the bathroom when she'd just stepped out onto the floor, creating puddles. No mat, they'd never got round to having one. She'd slipped as he'd grabbed for her, run his finger up her thigh with this intense look to him. She'd seen what he'd be capable of so she had to warn them. The friends were simpletons, looking with round-eyed innocence, as if they hadn't heard that fathers did that. But she couldn't dwell on what they thought, it was something she had to get over and done. She couldn't even afford the wish that life would be different, that the dad would be, that her mum wouldn't look so girly and wasted all at once the way she did, grey hairs in the thinning blonde. She cuts with the little nicking blade, lets the vileness out with her stream of blood. All washed away, better then. Miss Midlands Heartlands sitting under grey skies as rain comes on.

BEAUTY QUEENS

Dierdre's queasiness has passed with the whoosh of fresh wind which is coolish on her skin, allowing her to breathe, letting her mind settle. However unwelcome in other ways, it's relieved her. And that's good 'cause she wants to make the best of this day, she wishes the photographers would get here to take the pics, it's getting so dark suddenly, seems like night coming down. The wind carries a splash or two of rain onto her arms, shape of a tear, shape of flattened pear drops. Becoming Miss Night and Day Pharmaceutical for the second year running, such a triumph, nobody'd believed she'd do it, but she knew she would, was looking good that day, hardly needed to do a single thing, just came to her, came so easy. Good she's having this second time, it'll be her last. Dierdre thinking about Keith, the bad timing of splitting up like that, the way they had. But it had to be so, he was untrustworthy when it all came down to it, not the kind of guy she could settle for, even if he had've left his wife. Deirdre, her eye on the balustrade for firm focus, too realistic to paint the past in as anything better, too proud for regret, imagining herself as the axle of a wheel, the shiny silver hub of it. The wheel's rolling round and round, though she at the centre is still. She needs a decent place, her first priority whether she has the baby or not. She's been too unsettled in her life so far, with her parents dying and her living with different relations and once in care. Too much movement's just not in her nature. She knows that, but sometimes it's hard to get what you need. She catches sight of Candy's arm with its diamanté bangle, very retro, Candy lifting up her hand to wiggle the bangle backwards and wedge it far up towards her elbow, because it keeps sliding down. Sort of bangle that would look right on a long black glove, like on the *Breakfast at Tiffany's* posters you keep seeing now. Audrey Hepburn with a cigarette holder held at an acute angle, the bangle right there, part of the picture. The film's years old, Dierdre's never even seen it, but it's an image everybody knows. It seems eternal. Amazing that.

Shereen also sees the bangle go up and down Candy's arm many times, sees it distantly without thought, she's wondering whether she'll leave home or flit with her folks. Can she bear to do this yet again? Phil wants her to move in, of course. But could she really live with Phil and his laughter, which she knows by instinct has nothing to do with amusement or pleasure, but is simply a device to stop her in her tracks? She knows she should be steering clear. The temptation though! Thought of the house and no more money worries, he'd be at work, she'd have the run of the place. Wicked. Thought of being out on the town, here there and everywhere, and he's lavish, he's certainly that. A lot to be throwing away. And if she goes with her folks, what'll she have to put up with? The night-time bathroom gropings of her dad. She can't protect her mum forever from knowing the worst, and whatever other reason would she be going for? Makes her shudder, she nearly jolts her tiara right off her head just thinking of it. She's old enough to get out and make the break, but it's scary, and the thought of her leaving her mum alone with him gives her a pain. Then a harder streak flashes through her, after all her mum married him, and she could leave, there's nothing to stop her but cowardice. Shereen sees the diamanté sparkle but thinks of nothing, her mind's spinning off somewhere, she gives a quick darting glance at the little neat wound on the inside of her arm near the top, to ground herself.

Candy's decided to change her name to Kandi. The kicking leg of the K, sending off that little i-ball to infinity, a virtual universe, a movie screen. The dot of the eye is her being transported to somewhere else, all her hope's in that. *Kandi*, she says, feeling the shape of the name with her tongue, the name that's going to do it all for her, gonna take her there. As things stand she's feeling disheartened, the weather such a let down. How could it rain on her day, the one that was to be perfection. It's gone cold suddenly, too, Dierdre's searching her bag for her jacket, Shereen is shivering openly. For Kandi the worst aspect of the weather is the wounding of her self-esteem. The world seems to be saying she's of very little consequence after all. It hurts. Seeing the scattering crowd makes her feel abandoned and fairly hopeless. She stares at the bangle, its diamond glitter and wink as she shakes it back up her arm from the wrist. You can't wear just one bangle on its own, she suddenly thinks, there should be a whole bunch together. Though she doesn't know where she'd find any more like this one, because the fact is she stole it, and it was the only one in the box. Maybe the rest could be plain gold or silver, they don't have to match. But anyway, she didn't really steal it, she couldn't resist having it for her day of days, that was all. She'll be putting it back tomorrow, when she goes to Melda's, so what's the worry. Melda's her next-door-neighbour, she's eighty years old and can't see that well. Kandi goes round and sits with her, reading aloud all the captions under the photos in Melda's film-star album. She'd taken the bangle from Melda's box when Melda was dozing. Sneaky-sneaky. She feels a little bad, but why? It isn't stealing or anything like that, far from it. If she'd asked, Melda would definitely have lent the bangle. Kandi wouldn't have wanted to ask because she doesn't like anybody else knowing what she wants. And this kind of ignorance is also the spirit of things she likes for her own actions, she likes doing what she does easily without thinking, keeping awareness to a minimum. So she took the bangle without really dwelling on it, saying vaguely to herself it would be there as usual tomorrow, without Melda being any the wiser. Melda was dead keen on that bangle, it had its own special box. But still, what harm was there? Kandi's wide-narrow lips come together briefly then draw apart.

Tomorrow, Dierdre is to make her decision. She still doesn't know what she'll do. Sometimes she knows it's to be an abortion, then it changes, so how can you call that knowing? And same thing the other way, she's already half chosen the baby stretchsuits quite a number of times. She's afraid that when the time comes she'll just act on impulse, hopefully though it will only seem like an impulse, beneath the surface it may be the thing she really wants, she'll be making the serious choice. Anyway, she's going to stick with what she chooses, it's her way. She's feeling a bit down now, it's such a weight to be living under. But maybe she knows all along what she's really going to do, and the rest is just some kind of game, the kind of game that Shereen and Candy are heavily bound up in which she, Dierdre, normally doesn't have any time for. Whatever happens it's the end of the beauty queen scene. Time to get out now, whatever else is true, she's reached the point, she'll be twenty-five. Sitting in this bandstand in the grey of the rain, she pictures baby stretchsuits, sees herself pulling the tiny items out of their packets one by one, imagines guiding awkward tender arms and legs into the right little gaps.

Shereen's hardly registering the rain. She's remembering how she'd had Dell staying, last November. They were going to a club, Friday night, Dell had come back home with her from work. They'd been posing in a mirror together as though for an album cover. But Shereen had to move away, she'd been afraid Dell would see the little red nick just down near her shoulder, her latest cut mark, horrifyingly visible. She'd had to give Dell the rundown on her dad of course, nothing to that anyway, it was just what she did, like smiling in a beauty contest. The damp murky house though, she'd become aware of it through Dell's eyes, she'd felt embarrassed. Nothing going for it, not even a bath mat, and you had to put your naked feet on that cold grainy floor. Dump of a house squeezed in a swampy bit of ground between the trading estate and railway, forgotten looking, on a road going nowhere or nowhere very much. Dell'd had a funny look. Maybe not as much as horror, but certainly disbelief. They'd stepped down into her parents' bedroom because that was the way you got to the closet where Shereen's stuff was. Sharp frosty feel to the air, and a dark-at-four-thirty look to things, but a beam of light coming in from a streetlamp just by the window. By her parents' bed were two china chamber pots because the toilet was out in the yard and where else did you go at night, even if it was the year 2007? Full to the brim, they were. Two stagnant yellow pools with a sheet of thin toilet paper floating on the pee like lily-pads in moonlight. Shereen and Dell had just stood there for a second or two, then stepped over them, nothing was said. Shereen couldn't have friends who felt the need to say things, there was too much she didn't want to be reminded of. But later, after the club, when she was home again, lying in her bed, she'd touched the latest secret sore place. It was from that place all the bad things had poured, relieving her, the hard desperate look in her dad's eye when Dell had been sitting on the one unbroken chair downstairs in her skin-tight leopard-print skirt, the unfunny laugh of Phil which she'd heard so many times the previous night because she'd argued with him when he'd scorned to wear a condom, the joint collected pee of her parents. She'd touched at the sore, it was hurting, but still it was hurting in a way which helped, and then when she'd touched it enough and it had started to heal, it was as if her troubles faded too.

Kandi smoothing down her gloss brown hair, settles her silver headband, pretending the wind isn't disruptive—why see things the way they are when you can think them better. This would be Kandi's motto, if she had one. She smiles out again at the empty field with that mouth of hers, her best feature despite its crooked waywardness, it draws you. That pondering charisma she has, it's all centred there. Never sure where you are with her, her mind's somewhere else and the deliberations of her mouth are reminding you of that.

Dierdre says, 'Oh, sod this rain,' for the three of them, and they stare out over the balustrade across the now deserted recreation ground. A wasteland.

'What a sorry sight we are,' Dierdre thinks, and, 'Well, if that isn't life for you.' When she'd left home this morning she'd found a tiny gold medallion lying in the grass verge just by her car. She'd put it in her pocket for good luck. Tomorrow, before she makes her decision once and for all, she's going to drive out to the Lickey Hills and flip the medallion in the fountain. She'll wish to be shown the best way forward. Right now, in her mind, she's sitting in the middle of a train, the front coaches and the back ones are splitting off and going their separate ways. Like Candy and Shereen. But she's the one headed for the main destination, the proper one that's advertised on the departures board. This gives her an uplifted feeling, even though the place she's making for is only in the

GOD OF THE PIGEONS

real world of her own experience, Coventry or Wolverhampton or Birmingham New Street, and no more romantic than that.

Shereen hates the flitting. She knows why they'll do it, it's debts run up in the town, the rent on the house hasn't been paid in a while, the phone's cut off already and they're about to be cut off in everything else. Always the same story anyway. Every couple of years it's always happened, for as long as Shereen can remember. She thinks of leaving home and feels afraid. How will she manage? There's always Phil who can't get enough of her, wants her to move in. It's tempting though she's afraid of that laugh of his and of what's behind it, what's lurking there and never said, a kind of advance warning of how things will be. She realises she'll have to be constantly fawning and playing up to him, making the sort of squashy tongue smiles men go for. Maybe she can move in with him just till she gets sorted. Course there's nobody she can talk to and Shereen's too secretive anyway.

Kandi's changing her name to Holly, she wants to get right away from what's familiar. Even Kandi ties her down because somehow there's always Mandy there in the background dictating her life moves and the way she feels. Holly is a glitzy kind of name, she thinks of it as short for Hollywood, this gives her a successful feeling. She thinks of the crimson glisten of holly berries and the shiny green of the leaf. The berry is dynamic and red, the leaf is powerful with pointed prickles. An image of herself that's definitely pleasing, she curls her wide lips up into a new kind of grin to no one. Doesn't matter there's no recipient, she's just practising.

The sky's gone navy and black, rain's falling in a single sheet. Drumming sound of that sheet against the thin wooden bandstand roof. Drips and puddles are everywhere in next to no time. Here the three of them are, beauty queens, posing in a scene of desolation. Holly lets out a scream, she can't bear having her daydreams traduced like this, and the three of them leap up from the red velvet chairs and huddle tight together in the centre of the circular space. The bangle slips off Holly's wrist and rolls along the slatted floor, disappearing into a crack. They all see it happen but none of them can say where it's gone. Diamanté twinkle as it rolls, then nothing. Holly's on her knees scrabbling on the wet splintery wood, but there's no trace of it. The wind dashes against them in a squall, blowing wet paper wrappers, empty cartons, sodden bits of this and that light enough to travel. The beauty queens look out across the space where there's nothing to be seen moving at all now except the flap of awnings on the abandoned fete stalls, discarded takeaway packaging, the flight of plastic bottles. Buoyant. But Holly's back on track now with her own amended version of reality. She visualises the shift of debris as though through a camera's eye, then superimposes her own smiling image on the screen. Everything else fades down to nothing. If this were a movie it would make the perfect ending.

MAKING DRACULA

PRE-TEXT:

Two men from the video shop hold a bony little guy against a wall.

'You can't get away, mate,' one of them says.

'Okay, okay,' goes the guy, shrinking back from the glare of a streetlight. 'So it was a mistake. Calm down, won't you.' His hands fumble with a shabby wallet taken from his pocket. The hands shake.

'Now get out of here,' the other man tells him, taking hold of the money.

'And don't come back, you scummy bastard.'

The bony guy leaps like a rabbit that's seen a sudden bolthole. But will they really let him go? Kohl-rimmed whitened eyes, mouth of mucous red all a shiver. Will they? He skulks off, finds shadow, feels humiliated. For these terrors and temblings he'll make somebody pay.

DIALOGUE:

Thick yellow fog, dense, obscuring things. Feels total, feels like somewhere you'll never get out of. Feels forever as a lost world. But he's at home in the twilight, his tongue licks the lostness into shape in his mouth. It comes out as words: 'We can't go on.' He casts his eyes down now, low, as if suffering. Wow. He hasn't tasted anything as good since . . . *Hwaar*. His sigh coming out like a painful breath—his own personal reconstruction of the sound of sorrow. 'I just don't feel the right way about you.' Said tenderly for maximum knife-twisting effect, pain and regret, all the sort of stuff he wants to bring *out* here. Because, he's an okay person. There's a pause as he thinks through the part of a hesitating

MAKING DRACULA

decent guy Then he goes in for the kill. Sincerity precedes polish, he squeezes up his lips into a puckered moue. It's a fucking piss-take.

'And you. If you're truthful', he goes, 'you'll admit you don't feel right about me either. Am I correct?' He asks this gravely, experimenting with fatherliness, as he tastes the sense of failure, the impotence conjured up by the words. As he tastes the sense of loss.

And from across the table he hears Debbie sigh too. *Hwooh.*

How come he knew he'd reach her with this sincere patter. Just the thought of sincerity makes him want to puke and fall about at the same time. It makes him cringe.

Silence for a bit, then she says, 'I s'pose you're right.'

Acquiescence, wow. His heart's pounding with joy. Fuck, what a taste, what a glory, what a complete piss-take.

'I have tried, I really have, but you see it's so difficult when . . .'

What the fuck? He resents her tone of voice, reasonable, and there's this almost crisp efficiency. He's not fucking 'aving it. No, no, it's a bit of blood he wants. Blood. Pure and simple. Just that. The taste of it. Who's she to come out with this voice of reason? 'Shit!' he bursts in acidly with. End of story, cut the crap. Fuck her detailed explanations. Drooling heavily at the tits of the passing waitress. To show Debbie a thing or two, he rides roughshod across her last remaining vanity. If it is Debbie. He can't be expected to remember.

'We're not compatible.' He spits the words out, angry end-game style.

CHARACTERISATION:

A punch into air, doesn't want to hear one word more. End! End of story, end of the line. End of everything. Feels restless irritation, lights a fag, puffs out into heavy smoky atmosphere. Calms down somewhat when he sees this tear on Debbie's cheek. Or someone's cheek. Any cheek will do for this tear. Tear glistening through fog. Yes, calmer.

'We can remain friends, I hope,' he says, successful. He's wrestled the role of reasonable one away from her. It's fucking *his*. His role! She's s'posed to grovel and beg. That's the part she should be playing. And he gives a round and animated chuckle, though to say, though to say, 'Course we will.' Him being him being blokey.

'I, er, I don't know. I . . . What do you think?' Debbie's voice has turned self-doubting, weak; he's made her feel dull and unsexy and she hates herself because it matters.

'Whatever you like,' he goes. Mister Patronising. 'Whatever's easiest for you.'

He's taken on the style of a judge summing up now, sitting squarely in his chair and enjoying the lostness in her eyes, all the ruined confidence. He sits squarely, his heart's a tiny mechanism racing, even dancing. Self love, valid appreciation of his own astuteness, he's extracting a bit of emotion out of all this and it's a thrill, a blissful excursion. Sweet agony of her pain for him to feed off. Oh, wow, he's close to ecstasy. Eeeeee. The joy of it.

'What d'you mean, *friends*?' this Debbie unexpectedly asks him, and his eyes go black. He yawns. Maybe he'll fuck her some time if she's nice to him, but not now, no. He looks at his watch. Shit, it's nearly morning. He hates this bitch, whatever her fucking name is. All sour-breath, questions and desperate eyes.

'I gotta go.'

LOCATION:
The driver of the night bus won't accept his out-of-date pass. He rifles through his pockets for the fare. The eyes of the other passengers all glare at him with hatred for holding things up. He slinks to the back of the bus and sits in a trembling rage, sits huddled all the way to his stop. 'Fuck, bastard,' he mumbles to the smeared window through which he can see nothing except a trickle of water down the glass. Rain. Rain.

UNDER-TEXT:
Back in his favourite club, narrow beady eyes of him, fixed on the rump of the waitress. Fixed. Sharp animal stare of his which definitely says, 'I'm gonna eat you.'

MAKING DRACULA

His gaze riding with her, in all her undulations across the tables. Him right there, eyes of a ferret, thinking himself a rare killer of hearts, or at least a breaker. Keeps saying under his meaty stinking breath how he'd bloody bite into 'em, tear 'em up, toss 'em out and leave 'em for dead. What else would you do with hearts? The arse of the waitress, the focus for his bitter dreams.

' 'Ere,' he says.

He's one of those musicians nobody can place. It's always said about him though, 'Ya know, he used to play with, er . . .', which is something to get by on in the circles *he* moves in, esp. with *les bitches*. What he's up to mostly is teaching all the dumb little bimbos he can lay that he's free and they can't own him, and he likes a bit of a struggle before their necks flop soft. And there's always plenty of candidates for the part assigned them. It's ferrety tyrant time down at the club. It's him, who d'ya think, doing the assigning.

' 'Ere,' he goes to the waitress, assertive little heart-breaker that he is. As he holds up his glass for a refill, his eyes puffed out with this notion he has of himself as hero, priest and fool, and bad-man. ' 'Ere.' He's dreaming how when the waitress goes into the ladies' room he'll slip through the door, darkly. Like a shadow. Before she can speak he'll place his hand sideways between her legs, poke into her cunt with fingers, teeth and cock. So he dreams on. Dreams the smell of her crevices, her sap and inner red.

'We're closing,' the waitress says coldly, her eyes and mouth falling sideways in dislike. And he trots out surreptitiously. No murmur of dissent.

STRUCTURE:

'You're seeing *her*!' Emma's mouth draws in tight with hurt. He looks in some disdain at her soft-fat body and gives her a smile that's ferret-like, tiger-toothed.

'You're getting too clingy,' he accuses, pulling on his trousers, running up the zip with taunting emphasis.

GOD OF THE PIGEONS

'I'm entitled to know what's going on.'

He's furious, and at the same time slick with power. 'You want me to hit you,' he informs her, drawing on mainstream dialogue themes.

Malign pleasure flicks across his mouth. He sees these delicious movie clips of himself tying her down and piercing her with a sharp instrument, overriding her will. *His* is the will that matters. He wants her to goad him and cry and plead for mercy which he will not give. It goes without saying, he will not. It'd be cool to beat her to a pulp and then fuck her. If he could be bothered. If he really had the energy to use her up and defy her and overcome her.

'Oh, fuck yourself,' he suddenly says, wanting to fade away as mist through the gap under the door.

'You're a pervy bastard!' Emma shouts, and a bit of pre-ejac seeps out of him unexpectedly.

Yeah, that's more like it. He's getting a bit of a buzz from the accusation, and it's almost making him feel like staying to put his punishment into effect. But he pulls on his coat anyway, saunters to the door, says, 'Ring me.' It's cooler, this is a re-re-make, after all; it's what's in the current script. He goes staggering down the stairway without emotion, but in the street sees sun glinting in the gap between two blocks of flats. This makes him run, his sharp little body hunching forward, his squinting eyes kept low. Must get home.

'Hey, you!' a voice booms so close to his ear he quivers like a whipped dog as he tries to steep himself in darkest shadow. This sudden fucking light blazes full into his red-rimmed eyes, highlighting the bloodshot mess of them, making him wince.

'I'm talking to you,' the voice sneers. 'Christ, you're in a state, man. What you on?'

He tries giving a quaking smile of appeasement to get himself out of this, but can't seem to stop it coming out as a smirk. There's an anxiety creeping in. They make him keep on re-doing it, say they've got to get the whole thing right.

MAKING DRACULA

'Nothing,' he blurts out at last, apologetic, shoulders hunched, even aware himself of his own sad image.

'Get outa here. Get home,' the policeman barks, and he, a wretched little wafer of an antihero, slips off wordless into the maze of flats which rise before him like gigantic tombstones.

His POV.

PLOT:

'We can remain friends,' he goes blandly to Debbie, Emma, Sue, whoever, but his eyes, of course, are somewhere else. He's saying inwardly—What a line, a laugh, a piss-take—as their faces fade away like soap bubbles, smack, smack, smack. No shortage of bimbo replacements. He's Mister Popular with a vengeance. Always that.

Used to play with, er, whassat band, ya know—does him a few favours, good image and that. Pouncing and puncturing, taking such trophies as occur. Say, he might drag an earring from the earlobe of his lay, she'll scream, the whore; there'll be bloody traces over the gold. Fantasy of his. He drinks it in, image sticks with him. Nah, he being a *musician like*, has no trouble scoring. Drama of the coming dawn, he's streaking home, all no-emotion. Gothic grey intensity of the visuals; the music pounds.

UNDER-TEXT 2:

'Ere. Hero in the night café, rat-arsed by now, lad to the last. See in his eye how he dubs himself king of all he touches—these soft-minded women he favours are wanting to win, or at least to not be lost, so they're giving in entirely to his self-delusions. A good fuck (Only *good*?) Shit no, he's the best fucking fuck. Truth is, they'd pay any price for such a fuck as he can give 'em. Gagging for 'im. He and the latest lay in bed; it's wild. And he'll be telling her he's a superstar; not wanting to leave out any of the superlatives from his self identity. Unowned and free and brilliant, and he has the best cock, plus enchantment, going for him—oh, yes. Plenty of that commodity, and evil. He has evil going for him. He's a magic-man, and he's even imperfect—in the most flattering and desirable way of being so that ever was, a course—only thing he lacks is modesty, only other thing he lacks is a brain, only other, other, other, other, other . . . Yawn.

Anyway, governed by mists and hot night flushes, he's put in charge of the movie mags where he finds he's already been entered big time. He's listed as hero and antihero in as many ways as can be thought of, covering his arse on all sides. And they're *still* asking for him, asking for more.

ACTION:
New grey night, he struts in the town. Having taken on board what's called charm, for the intention of scoring with a bimbo, he slides by, serene, in his fox's hat, sleek winsome trill to that voice of his, and with a heady smell. Overpowering animal going for the kill. He'll tear your heart out, even when he doesn't mean to eat you, being fond of sport. In the chippie he sneaks a curry sauce meant for the guys in front.

'You sad fucker,' they say to him. 'You're a dead man if you ever come back here.'

He's legged it before they've expressed even a quarter of their disgust.

DENOUEMENT:
It's getting early, he's starting to lose the sense of things, starting to droop and that. This is what always happens. It has to be written into the script this way. It's at the core of his self identity. There wouldn't *be* a Dracula without this inbuilt terror of the dawn. Even so, they're not about to let him be. Katie phones him and says regretfully, 'Is it really over?' her voice half swallowed by the choke-up in her throat. 'But I love you.'

To cut things short he tells her she's shit in bed. And it's true to say she's quickly shamed and then can't speak at all. She's further stymied by the truckloads of self-loathing she's releasing, because, ridiculously, even though he's a horror story, she finds herself wanting to apologise. It's so crap and corny but she keeps getting pulled in that direction.

MAKING DRACULA

She's frustrated, can't think of anything better to say than *sorry*. Tears come. The moist sound of her sorrow brings him to a bit, makes him pant a bit. There's the smell of blood in it. *Blood*. A reviving thing. He'd like to lick it out of her, drop by glistening drop, and this is the closest he'll come to feeling life as we know it, to feeling emotion of any kind. As *she* droops *he* strengthens, dead-and-alive devil that he is.

But I love you. Oh piss-take. Who writes these things?

Anyhow, it's getting early, he's got to take cover—he's coming over groggy, feels the need. Streak of light in the sky and all that. Oh, shit. Needs to get back, fuck, fuck everything, what a life, eh, he's shattered, to say the least. Get home, get to sleep, be out for the count till nightfall. Start again.

RACETRACK

Henry hates people
who try to fool you, with Honeymoon eyes, smart arses, those with something to hide, and they're pretending to be nice, only pretending, he himself lives up on the 4th floor, but these are the sort that live in basements, murky bastards, and then they try to put on this show for you, they waltz out now and again in fancy dress, on a Sunday, to fool you, to keep you happy, he says all of this showing-off stuff is shit, they might as well give up, he's *thirty-eight*. When he was younger, well he might've got sucked in by 'em, thought they were okay, then when they couldn't keep it up, the truth would've slipped out, the horror. All that nice-smiley stuff being put on to deceive him. Like when he was a kid and people got dressed in their best on a Sunday, in his family they did, and if you didn't know any better you'd think that's the way they were, but it wasn't true, that was only the way they were on a Sunday, he wouldn't let anybody dress up in Sunday clothes ever if he could help it, course nobody does now, but the pretence still happens all the same. Sunday-best eyes. Makes him uneasy just to think of, makes him insecure, because those people they're not really what they're telling you they are, they're something very different. Trying to deceive but he's not having it, he fucking isn't, no not himself, they needn't try anything on. And at weddings, they particularly dress themselves up at weddings, trying to be different from how they are. Disguises. Him, he's steering clear of that sort, he likes the ones who say what they mean and don't try, they certainly don't try, to do anything clever, and they're not got up special for a Sunday but stay what they are on a weekday and if he doesn't care for 'em because they're just a Monday-morning type, wet-like, grey, he can keep out of their way and nobody gets hurt. If that's the weather, pretending it's all sunshine only makes for trouble. They

RACETRACK

might be a Tuesday, settling in, no side to 'em, he can take em or leave 'em, or a Wednesday, given over, totally accepting they're in the middle of a thing and can't get out of it. He's escaped from Wednesdays, all Wednesdays of this kind, he himself, so he'd know to steer clear of 'em. No, what makes him laugh is the idea they might think they could really take him in, or it makes him angry, sometimes it *does* make him angry. He himself isn't trying to put one over, this is what he is, it's that or nothing, and if the best they can be is a Thursday pay day, or a Friday coming up to the weekend, they should make the best of it, and it's fair to say that he himself is what he is all of the time, everbest. And this is also the true story of how Henry comes to be on medication.

Henry thinks of himself
as a kind person, now and then an angry person, true, angry when slimeballs try to pretend they are other than what they are. He hates the thought of them all fake and showy, trying to slip something across, sidling up as if everything's fine, then springing the truth on him, trying to pin him down, trying to hold onto him, make him eat dog dirt, but he's faster than they are and he won't let them do it, you fucking bet he won't. But he has to keep on moving or they'd get him, they'd get right to him, pull him down, suck him under, he'd be finished but he ain't ever gonna let a thing like that happen, Christ no, because he's faster than they are, and he is this naturally, doesn't have to pretend, never had to pretend, he is what he always is, fastest and best, he believes this of himself, believes such a thing is possible. Other people would like to stop him, maybe they would like to stop him once and for all, but no, he'll keep on moving, keep on being fast. So fast they may miss him altogether if they happen to be looking away when he is passing, in which case he'll come back to where they are, he'll have to, he's not about to be ignored. Wants to let 'em know he's fast and see he can't be stopped, he can't be stopped, so he'll pause just long enough for em to get a sight of him if there's a doubt, then off. Men as well as women, at heart

they're all bastards. He sees himself *too right* as someone who has rumbled the rest.

Henry doesn't like straight lines
which go down as well as up, straight and vertical, so he runs round in circles, runs rings round other people, keeps on going. The round. He starts and finishes his day at St Pancras Library making sure all is in order here. Morning and Evening. Are the books present on both occasions? Are the videos and DVDs, the language courses, the newspapers, the information packs for Camden residents? Yes, they are, they're all here, so Henry can carry on running, he doesn't have to blow his brains out today, a Thursday. Setting off up the Euston Road, direction of Great Portland Street, coffee at the tube station, small squeezed-up café, not many seats so he can't find one. This suits him, it's hard to be seated, for Henry it is. He's relaxed today, which means he can stop long enough for a coffee if he doesn't sit down to have it. Stands near the exit, looks out at rush hour crowds, with cold water in his coffee so's he can drink it quickly, but can't keep still even so, just can't, can Henry, shifting from this foot to that foot all the time he's drinking. Then off out the door, quick as light. Feeling restless, the coffee making him palpitate, making his head throb faster. To Baker Street tube, his fave for coffee because at this café there are *no* seats. He just stands at a round plastic marble table, the only near irritating thing being that everybody else is standing too. So that when he goes he won't have so much of a head-start and they could be after him, they could catch him up easier, but shit, no they won't, cause he's the FASTEST and they better not forget it, he'll be safe. He shifts his feet more, palpitates more, then he's off.

Henry has this fixed pattern
that he has to keep to, so he always takes the same route through Regent's Park to Chester Road, runs down the same strip of grass each time, between the walkway and the borders, goes to the Inner Circle, and when he gets there he just keeps on running. This is HIS place in the

RACETRACK

whole universe, it is Henry's place, like a home here to him, he's devoted. Runs round it and round it and round it till lunchtime, doesn't have to think. At lunchtime the alarm on his watch goes, time to go off to the café in the Park to get a sandwich, which he can eat while he's on the move, must eat the sandwich while he's on the move. Doesn't sit down in the café, or outside at one of the tables, what, couldn't settle enough for that, would feel too threatened, as if he were being pinned down somewhere, being taken advantage of, trapped in a weak moment, hampered. That's what they'd like to do, all the bastards out there, there in the horrible world outside the Inner Circle, his own and special place, where he's safe. Pity other people have to be here at all, but he tries to think it empty, and this'll have to do him, he can't deal with the problem of how to get rid of them, he's worked it out and knows it can't be done, because even if he blew up the lot of 'em, more would come. That's the thing, more would, he knows it, so it's not worth the bother. There's too many of 'em for him to deal with, a whole world full. Can't deal with 'em, can't! Oh fuck, fuck 'em. But they can't catch him, that's what counts, and look at 'em, they haven't even understood they're walking along on his personal RACETRACK. So stupid, and he, he's running rings right round 'em, they don't even know it. He runs, slowing down, biting off a bit of his sandwich, prawns in mayonnaise, same as everyday; teatime takes a standing break for tea and for a pee, then carries on till 5 o'clock. Time to go to the library, to dust the books, to tidy them up on the shelf, check the alphabetical order is being kept to, to refold the daily newspapers when they've been creased, when they've been creased in the wrong places, ignoring the centre fold.

Henry goes to pieces
the next day, a Friday, because of a barrier, a barrier that's blocking off the Inner Circle, at Chester Road, what'll he do, he's held up here at this barrier, he's in a sweat. Could he duck under, his feet itch to carry on, he must carry on doing what he always does, he can't stop, can't stop for a barrier, just a barrier, that can't stop him, but the police are here, they're

watching him as he runs on the spot, what now, what should he do? He thinks quickly, he thinks on his feet, won't let the bastards defeat him. Runs to the left, zigzagging through grass and bushy bits, gets mixed up in a ball game, does a detour because of a fence, does a detour because of a dog, sweats heavily, says 'shit!' quite a few times. Trying to get to York Gate, so's he can get into the Inner Circle *that* way. Can't be done, there's still a barrier, work's being carried out on the road, you can't get into the Inner Circle now and if you're in it you can't get out. Wishes he was in it but he isn't. What can he do, what can be done? He doesn't find out how long this state of things is going on for, what he does do is sits down and cries, hits a policeman, gets arrested, and this is the true story of how Henry came to be on medication. Now he is on medication and his life is like this:

Henry hates people
who have a hidden agenda, feels freaked by the idea there could be something else than what you can see, things covered up, he can't cope with that, he Henry always is what he is and no other. EVERBEST, and this, all of the time. Gets up, goes to the library and checks the books, runs down the Euston Road, drinks his coffees at tube stations, hops from one leg to the other, here's the park, the same Inner Circle which there always is, good, he's used to it, he doesn't have to stop and think, life is a racetrack. There has been a change for the better, he's moved flats, gone up a level, gone to the fifth floor, trying to get far away from the basement, far as possible, higher is happier. Why should there be a basement, he can't stand basements, how could anybody want to live in a basement, having basement thoughts, having a basement personality. People, they can be weird, but not him, no, they wouldn't get him in a basement, he's going higher, going higher, up into the air. He could have been a lift attendant, in another life, in a life where he could keep still, where he could sit on a stool in the corner, just the one corner, all of the day, except that he couldn't have anyway because lifts go down as well as up, they will always have to go to the basement, the household

RACETRACK

department, he wouldn't have any of that. At home he is minimalistic, that's the way he has to have it, nothing to get in the way of him, nothing to pin him down, he can jog from room to room, finally he can sleep on the floor, on his camping mattress that rolls up, it rolls up, the camping mattress, so he can put it away, in the built-in wardrobe, with his running shoes, have all of the space empty, and to himself.

BATMAN

Weekends means back to the leather look. Fantasy and fun are what John and April would say they're about. Feeling cool going shopping on Saturdays. Black groovy jackets, tight black trousers silver zipped.

John spends his work days below street level, packaging catalogues to order, scurrying, making zigzags from table to desk to door in the musty semi dark. Life in the warehouse, with corrugated cardboard, rolls of brown paper, endless spools of sticky tape. A dim daily life experience, all very dim. He'll scurry here and then there across the floor of the basement, leaving tracks crisscross in the dust. Lunchtime. Sits at the bottom of a staircase eating crisps and a wholemeal salad bap washed down with fizzy water. Evenings he goes home to his wife. They watch TV together and rarely disagree about the channels. His wife is called April because she was born in that month.

There's a dry-finicky neatness about the two of them, even their leathers have a careful newly-folded feel. A nice and tidy look. Well, that's *the two* of them, John by himself has a morose, gloomy quality crouching inside him, a deep half-hidden religious longing. But the atmosphere created when they're together isn't half so cheerless as April keeps up a stream of gossiping chatter which almost sounds like animated conversation. And they're not without a shared affection. Manifestation of John's feeling for April often takes the form of an avid non-sensual rubbing and chafing of her back and limbs. At such times her head bobs wildly and she's apt to lose breath, but she bears it with a grim smile, conscious that the display will soon give way to his habitual muteness and she'll be off the hook.

BATMAN

Sometimes a beam of self-awareness shines on all John's secrets, he sees so vividly his own special parsimonious enjoyment of life, observes his own dry-chafing expressions of affection and does not like what he sees. Deep inside a bubble of anger stirs. April is fairly bloodless though not to the point of anaemia. There *are* occasional bursts of inner heat, and she can be showery. A brittle scorched twig of irritability gone smudgy with rain. 'John,' she'll call out to her husband, quavery, shrill, red-eyed. She's moved by the need to share a grievance, and the very sound of her voice at such times brings that low bubble in him up to the level of his throat. Bitter juice, churning. Taste of anger.

They share their sparse ascetic kind of affection, buy useful items for the flat, eat scanty alcohol-free suppers, go to bed sleepy after a TV evening, never later than eleven on a working day as they're to be up spruce at seven. April has less romantic leanings than John, with his semi-hidden religiosity, which she dislikes. She'd have swept these vague cobwebby lingerings of his away if it'd been at all possible, with the latest efficient vacuuming equipment. But somehow, by some stealthy nocturnal instinct, he eludes her. Meanwhile his religious feelings have scarcely found form, let alone the power of expression. Inside him, John has a deep desire to be good and, what almost matches this in intensity, a deep desire to be saved. From all kinds of things—his inner turmoil, mainly, and from the kind of life he's living. Also he has this terrible fear of mediocrity. It's unvoiced, this fear, even to himself, but it's a driving force just the same. He has uneasy feelings when he looks into April's eyes sometimes, especially when she'll glance up suddenly in the middle of poring over her bank balances. There will be this special kind of silence in the room which seems to reflect April's absorption with her task. The expression in her eyes at such a moment, yes he's capable of hating that. To him it's the essence of the mediocre. He intuits the rows of figures. Left hand path, right hand path, and the balance. He wonders unhappily, whether April's eyes mirror his own. He thinks they do. This thought is the pits. Apart from the evil thick anger which sometimes enters his soul, and which is his alone, he himself has that same expression April has, he knows it, the bit of smirking meanness, but neat about the edges, moving towards blank. *Empty concentration* is how he thinks of it. He's seen that in the mirror sometimes when he's been looking at himself. But anyway, he feels protective towards April because of the way he sees her. Her characteristics, which are his too, he feels intensely private about, there must be no witnesses. He feels a huge loyalty towards her, could be moved to kill if somebody else voiced the same criticisms he has. As if April is a part of himself he's not really all that keen on, but for this very reason feels a burning need to defend. It's a kind of love. The two of them, part and parcel, could never leave one another, they're inextricably bound. And anyway he hasn't the slightest temptation to change anything about their lives. It's not even that he'll say he feels wrong about the way things are. At the same time he's clinging with obstinacy to his dark sweet inner need and his dreams of a saviour who will rescue him, lead him through the wilderness to some pure light.

It's April. It's April's birthday. John is wearing his tight black trousers and his leather jacket, April the same. He has to buy a birthday present. Skimpy, but not in the frivolous sense. Something functional, something that will be appreciated, be approved, something that will not be wasted.

The day is dry but April is definitely showery. No card has come from John's sister, Margot, April has snivelled and mooched about all the morning, her pale eyes wetly red. At the base of John's throat a flare of anger. Nothing in the second post. April's eyes get redder, John's skin burns with acidic fury against this negligent sister. Hearing April sniff, he's almost blind with a ghastly impotent rage.

Not flowers. *What can you do with flowers?* Something—he doesn't know what. It's lunchtime. They dissect a thin grey fish together and eat it with a sprig of parsley. In the afternoon he is to buy the present. The two of them are to drive into town together, to the store, then John is to go off separately and they'll meet up later on in the restaurant. This is the pattern they always follow.

BATMAN

If not flowers or perfume, then what? What?

They zip up their matching black jackets and go out, the afternoon is fragrant, white and blue, a fresh as new paint feel to it.

He so wishes to be good, it would be a comfort to do good deeds. Secretly he'd like to be a saint but knows his dark-blood anger works against him. Unsaint-like. He hates this imperfect part of himself which precludes the growth of sainthood. The bubble is vast and glutinous, it surges higher, higher, maybe is unstoppable.

They drive past the church: JESUS THE SAVIOUR. COME FORWARD TO JESUS NOW AND BE SAVED. April laughs airily at the words on the huge placard so as to minimize their impression on John's mind. The expanding bubble twists itself into a knot which tightens his stomach and then churns.

'Jesus the Saviour,' April sings in a light derisive voice, the inference in her tone being that she and John are in agreement over the absolute silliness of religion.

Sitting elbow by elbow in the little tinny car, black jacketed in unison. Snap-bone brittleness of their life. He, hating his anger, hating the sight of red eyes, hating equally the humdrum days and nights with their small, even-ticking reverberations, their predictable tears, their vapid smiles, hating the hating. Especially that. And wanting to be free of this whole sequence which defines and binds him. Wanting to be saved. He's close to despair.

And April, clinging desperately hard to the smooth veneer of daily concerns, intent on a life of total absorption by trivia, beyond the shadow of difficult questions.

'Don't spend too much on the present,' she reminds John. Not that she needs to, except that it's a thorough pleasure to her, this contemplation of sparseness. It's nearly as sweet as the high she gets looking through the increases in her savings account. Not quite though, for she can gaze at these columns of figures for a long time without getting in the least bored, feeling for once secure, full, unwhittled. An almost holy contemplation, the nearest *she* ever comes to experiencing spiritual emotion of any kind. When new *round* figures are reached it makes her sigh a delicious sigh. What a bliss, these whole seconds of luxurious happiness. Her reason for existence seems authenticated by these rows of printed numbers.

Neither John nor April can enjoy holidays, the embellishments of colour or luxury, or letting go. They seem made for one another in many ways, soul-linked in narrow complicity. April hints she'd be quite happy with gloves again, or she could go for socks. Socks, actually, are better as her gloves are not quite worn yet, also he once bought that suspect pair with a flower stitched onto the fronts. An aberration but still, he'd been a bit funny when they'd passed that church. You never knew.

'Socks, I could do with,' she trills as they speed through windy sunlight, the rising bubble darkening to sombre in the remote recess of his stomach linings.

April places her hand on John's arm. 'Margot might have sent me a card, just a card,' she says, tears brimming round her eyes like water lapping over pale fishes. His mouth hardens into two stiff whiskerish lines, he makes no sound.

In the store April goes to look at clothes, though she knows she'll never buy anything. She examines the labels and feels pleasure at what she'll be saving. John's inner bubble pulsates but it's netted in by a tight membrane which should keep it from breaking surface. In Lingerie he sees racks of black underwear spread out like dead butterflies, giving him a sense of nocturnal calm. He closes his eyes.

'Can I help you?' the assistant asks him.

He blinks at two rows of pearl-shiny teeth and shies away to Perfume, his body agitated, quivering. 'I'm looking for socks,' he calls back to the teeth, humbled, afraid of the dimensions of the woman's body, her cow-like head, domineering tits, flamboyance of her orange hair. Her eyes are insolent and unquelled. John scurries to the shadows of the stairwell. In the dull half-light he's able to recover. The quiet periphery of the landing isn't unlike the atmosphere of the packaging basement. He softens out, spreads his fingers. Then, re-animated, runs up the stairs taking two or three at a time. As he goes he's coming closer to sound. New sound. The chatter and clink of a tearoom. He sits near the top of the staircase in a nifty little corner, his arms extending forward like two stiff encircling wings, sits for a long time folded in upon himself and unmoving. At last he passes on, goes up to the doorway of the cafeteria.

A crowded room, grey with bright highlights, the uniformity flecked with the details of tiny things. He leans against the doorpost, notices very small scraps of colour. Buttons on coats, cherries on iced Bakewell tarts, mauve daisies on the side of a dress which wax and wane as the folds of material shift, a pale hand holding a teapot poised over a cup, a thin stream of brown liquid flowing down from the spout. He gasps. Except for the scraps and the windows, everything else is grey, and the chattering buzz seems dreary, never ending. It pulls him down. What if all the greyness were to seep into and over him and he could never be free of it? Panic. He holds his hand across his mouth. But no, no, the windows are good. The windows won't let the grey room get to him and drown him out. They're huge and shimmering, full of a strange yellow light. Tall, imposing windows, glass, semi-opaque. A church-like quality. Good windows full of light that seem to open up a world of possibilities. His spirits start to soar.

In the centre of the room he suddenly sees April, her narrow shoulders hunched forward over a magazine, her brown-mouse hair hanging limply against her neck. Having a cup of tea, waiting for a parcel of socks and no surprises. His heart lurches with pity and hatred for the two of them, for the bonds and life-chains which link them together so totally there's *no* breaking out. His throat, mouth, even eyes, are awash with liquid pain. There is no bubble left, it has smacked and gone leaving a stinging sensation like a trace of soap. He lets out a wild cry and half runs, half swoops towards her. She's already risen in her chair and it both pleases and frightens him to see that she's not smiling.

This is real then. It *must* be, for April always was an accurate mirror of their joint destiny. He's galloped up to her, has reached her, gripped her hard, has her way across the floor by now. Coming to the yellow light. Aware of passing very near to the moving mauve daisies, to one red cherry on white icing, to the sound of screaming. 'Shut the fuck up,' he hears and the words are so close he thinks they may have come from him. His hands are tight on April's bony frame. Bonds and chains. Bonds and chains. Inextricable. Colour gone, grey gone. Just the yellow, which is luminous, overpowering and without doubt the colour of glory. Window. It rises before them like a hand held up for silence at the beginning of a prayer. Window!

It's splintering and shattering and then they're out through the glass, their two black-jacketed bodies jerking through air like one projectile, figures harsh against the light. Two pale faces set as masks stark against sky, making towards earth, towards ending, two black jackets flapping like cloaks in the wind.

SEE YOU LATER, FRANÇOIS MARIE

What keeps me going is I have a secret friend. So though I make my way to the post office, nursing many bruises, I'm alright somewhere inside me. I'm sharing all of the hurt. Bruises of disagreement, mental bruising. Bruises and wounds. I lock them all inside myself and walk. I walk decisively, keep a cool head, keep my spirits up. And I'll try not to go under, even though nearly everybody's against me, pressing me down. Telling me this and telling me that but not supplying reasons, without revealing *reason*. *Because, because*, is all I can draw out of 'em. It makes me burn.

Them: *It's always been done like this. Everyone knows.*
Me: *But how do they, why do they?*
Because, because . . .
How do we know it's true?
Oh Angie.

Being realistic, no kind of discussion's about to happen, cliché is too entrenched in 'em. So I look at my friend and I see he's seen this and is saddened too and the burn goes right out of me. I'm starting to feel quite cool.

There's also Kevin, of course, I can talk to *him* quite a bit, other than that I'd be totally alone, wouldn't I. I'm fifteen and I'll tell you this much— the world's shite. Apart from Kevin and the Secret Friend, there's no one. At home there's the fog of television with its over-the-top colour, its incessant moan and drone. Eyes of the parents, accusing me. It would be frightening not to have any friend at *all*. At school, eyes of the teachers, just the same, groan of the class when I argue. But I have to do that, it's so essential. It hurts but it has to happen. This joyless thing, the clear argument. It's only joyless because of them, because of the fear they make me feel at seeing how alone I am. I hear my voice ring out in the classroom attracting a faint echo, soft sighs and whispers, a few rude noises. I'm telling you, it's a nightmare life. Why's there so much stuff I'm not supposed to think about?

I wrote a poem about dying. My father made exaggerated eyes to my mother, as if to say, *She's mad*. Getting a bit of fun out of it, he took the poem off to an aunt, and then a teacher. *She's mad*. His eyes with a veiled important look, as though he was on a special mission. And I could tell from this look he was secretly enjoying himself; that it was a moment of power.

Yes, I watch him closely and have come to see how much he wants to have power over me. Tryin to lord it, but slyly, covering his tracks. Sometimes he goes further, comes up with a bit of forcefulness like, *You'll have to have your hair cut. I've made an appointment*. But then he'll add it's because my hair's so untidy and he wants to help me look nicer. He's so good at making himself sound reasonable. Or he tries these annoying briberies like, *I'll take you to lunch, put on a nice dress*. My questioning of the idea, *nice* and inevitable refusal to go in anything but jeans leads to more of the *mad* talk. And he's so good at quick meaningful glances to whoever it is he's trying to turn against me, at the same time looking the part of well-meaning innocence. He'll put all the *well meaning* into his look for my mother, or for anyone else who happens to be there. But for me there's always the little private glint to let me know how much he's enjoying making me squirm. But this kind of gloating's all he gets. It isn't that much considering what he really wants is to control my way of thinking. He couldn't ever *do* that and he resents it. So he just has to try and get back at me in all these ways that are so exasperating. But they don't really touch me. Having said that though, I *am* hurting inside and I think sometimes I'd like to die because I can't imagine any way out of the life I'm living. It's all just one total agony. And then up pops François Marie. Things have become just bearable because of that.

SEE YOU LATER, FRANÇOIS MARIE

I go into my house, opening the front door as quietly as I can. Don't want to have any attention, do I. I'm level with the kitchen. Here the parents are, sitting at the table, with mouths chewing round and round, with TV-watching eyes. I can hardly bear to look at 'em. I slip past the kitchen door, my father makes a disparaging noise, my mother clucks. Sometimes I think I *am* mad, but shit no, I won't give way to such a thought. That's what he'd like me to do. And then, after I'd been broken down, I could cry and be forgiven and become *normal*. Real madness of course is not what he's talking about. He's trying to frighten me into submission, that's all, just wanting to see me soft-faced and smiling, going off shopping with my mum. Nothing bad.

'Why can't you be like other girls?' My mother chips in with.

'What d'you mean?' I say.

She does a kind of lax face as if it's too hard to put into words all my weirdness, at the same time looking comfortably aware the whole world would see it and be on her side, against me.

Are there people somewhere, anywhere, that aren't like this? Isn't there anyone out there who's a bit like me?

As I'm telling you, if it wasn't for François Marie It'd all be *madness* with a capital M.

Going down the road to the post office, feeling just this bit of brightening because I'll be seeing Kevin. He's a man as old as my father but he said to call him Kevin. I like him because we argue about the meaning of truth and what people have in mind when they tell you God exists. He takes me seriously, doesn't yawn or sigh or tell me to shut up. I'm full of other questions

'What is failure?' I ask Kevin.

He screws up his watery eyes. A few drops squeeze out of the corners, like tears. 'It's when you've started to do a thing and then you don't finish it.'

GOD OF THE PIGEONS

'But supposing on the way you saw a better thing? Would it still be failure or part of a wider possibility?'

I buy some stamps.

'Isn't it true Kevin, there's more than one way of looking at a thing?'

'Yes, of course there is,' he says.

'But Kevin, you know, nearly all the people I meet just believe fixedly in the one thing. And they haven't even thought it out. They're full of prejudice. All the people I know Kevin, seem to enjoy being blind.'

Kevin laughs a lot at this and shakes his head. His eyes screw up into nothing with the laughter. I do get this slight feeling sometimes he's humouring me a little bit for the sake of his own amusement. Now and then I'll catch him looking at me as though I'm a kind of entertainment. And a bad thing is that I've sometimes seen myself doing this wide-eyed naivety with him to gain his approval, seen myself being a bit precocious. To make him look and laugh, because I know it pleases him, whereas performance shouldn't come into things. It's the *ideas* that count. But no, I'm not gonna be to be too hard on Kevin, after all apart from François Marie, he's the only one I can talk to in any way at all.

And here I am, I'm walking along the High Street. I'm angry, I'm feeling down.

Because, because. It's all I keep on hearing. Yeah, so, the grass is green. I feel blocked off. Repeated walls of numbing silence are what I'm facing. Not that it's quiet in any way, all the people I know are full of burble and chat, ego stuff, empty crap. They're constantly flinging all their opinions around, never doubting I'll be agreeing with them or not caring a hoot if I don't, because who am *I*? I'm only a nut, in their books. But behind all the noise is a silence about things that should really matter. I have to say that at rock bottom, I feel so lonely. I'd like to have friends to talk to about the meaning of life but seriously, that isn't going to happen. I'm daydreaming but when I focus I see Delia who's in my class at school. Her frosty-sparkly lipstick. Watching her reminds me how alone I am. I can't get into this thing she's hot for, this boys/guys *go for it* abandonment, it

SEE YOU LATER, FRANÇOIS MARIE

doesn't feel right to me. She's hot on the trail of all this right now, has no ears for words. And anyway, guys are the one topic she'll get animated about. Music she'll tolerate, but it ends there. I can sense so clearly this moment as she wiggles her way forward that despite the youth and bright-eyed factors she's an almost identical person to my mother. So I don't make the mistake of saying to her, 'What are the limitations, Delia, of democracy as we know it?' Her peachy-pink lips push outwards, past me. You could say she's not politicised.

To the post office. Here I go now with my banner. But wait, *what do I mean by that?* My banner—well there isn't one really, and that's quite an important point. I don't believe in banners. But it's true to say I'm marching forward with *something*, a statement bursting up inside me, a flavour of a thought, or of many thoughts. I'm not entirely sure what all of them are. But as for the idea of a banner in itself... You have to be so careful about the language you use, even to yourself. I'm seeing now that banners are good for getting followers, for being easily identifiable and all sorts of shit. But a banner just isn't me, I don't have that kind of a mentality. A banner would embarrass me. Because there's always something more that needs saying and a banner is such a cutting-off thing, maybe not even getting near the main idea. Probably it will have a catchy slogan and it'll keep people happy, like a TV screen. It *is* a TV screen, though a static one. Held up in front of your face so you don't have to think for yourself. It's all done for you, all sorted. But if you weren't taken in by it and you *wanted* to think a thing out for yourself you'd say 'fuck off'. I say it. 'Caus there's no way I'm gonna be a passive recipient. I shout 'fuck off!' two or three times. Several people turn and look at me. Oops!

To the post office. I wave at Delia across the way. Life's so unfair really, I mean my parents would be that happy with Delia for a daughter and instead of her what they got was me.

There's a calm atmosphere inside, almost an echo. If I believed in ghosts I'd say there was a good chance there would be ghosts in here. I join the queue, count out my money for the stamps I'll need. In the end-but-one guichet I see Kevin. At this moment he's dealing with a customer, looking practical, not so much the intellectual as I think of him. He's adding up with a serious face as if his thoughts are all contained by what he's doing and there's nothing in reserve. This is somewhat alarming, but maybe there's an important lesson to be learned here — it's a bad idea to judge from appearances. I'm sure that inside Kevin there's a brain which makes him think sincerely about such questions as, 'But what is the meaning of meaning?' It's just that at some moments, when he's dealing with ordinary members of the public, it can be hard to imagine. I mean, like now, for instance, while he's sitting there with his mouth open, and a far away gluey-fishy look, calculating the price of twenty second-class stamps. And that's another thing, how can Kevin stand to do the job he's doing? I mean, there's not much scope in it for a thinking person, as far as I can see. It's a little frightening to think that somebody could end up in a nowhere corner of a nowhere town adding up stamps. Or is there a fatal flaw in Kevin which made this happen? Either way it makes me uneasy. I can't believe Kevin chose this as his destiny. Or maybe he'll move on and do something different one day. My brain can hardly handle that thought. Seriously strange to think of him somewhere else. I come to see that we sort of expect people to always be what we see them as, fixed in certain places like plants. *We* are the free ones, on the move through life and places, but other people are inseparable from where we've got used to seeing them. Double standards. What a tyranny. I must try not to fall into that way of seeing. I've never come across Kevin in the town, come to think of it. It'd be weird somehow to bump into him at the cinema or a café. But he can't exist under the counter in the post office, just popping up like a jack-in-a-box when customers appear. He must live somewhere and go away to that place. I realise I just don't know very much about him.

'Hello, Kevin,' I say when it's my turn. 'I was just thinking how we only see fragments of things, like other people's lives for instance and how easy it is to think you know all about them and what they are. And

SEE YOU LATER, FRANÇOIS MARIE

Kevin,' I say, before he can get a chance to digest this one, 'what would you say was the definition of *tyranny?*'

It's because there's usually only me and François Marie, the minute I see Kevin all the words that've been piling up in me come bursting out. A million questions I've got lined up for him when he's dealt with the ones in hand, when he's added up the stamps, weighed the parcels, told you what it costs to send stuff here, there and everywhere. Maybe after all he *did* choose this job, so his mind could be kept free for real thoughts. And when he gets absorbed-looking over trivial things in that way he has, it's just that he's slipping, life is getting to him, he's in danger of losing it. Maybe I could help Kevin to get a grip, move on to a more positive mental environment. Maybe Kevin has taken a few wrong turnings.

For a whole year I go to the post office, buy stamps and have discussions with Kevin over the counter. It seems as if it'll go on forever, and then some changes happen. The post office is closed for refurbishment for quite a long time, I leave school and get a job in an accountants' office. I make the cups of instant and carry them to the partners and the secretaries as they pore over columns of numbers in a way which makes me feel quite ill. *What a life!* No wonder the idea of Heaven was invented. *To encourage people to put up with this sort of awfulness without breaking out.* Something better is coming their way so it won't matter that much if they waste what time they have in the here and now. They're content to deceive themselves, I see the whole process quite clearly. I know I won't be able to stick it for long at this dump. I've learned how to be amenable and talk about fatness and fitness and clothes, but this is the precious-only life. Unlike the partners and secretaries I have this fear of squandering mine on trash. At home, in my room, I lie on my bed and fire questions at the wall, ask François Marie what is meant by *Liberty*.

It's a Saturday and I've gone into town. The recently refurbished central post office has just re-opened. It now has some metallic strips where the wood panelling used to be and features bits of smoked glass and a carpet.

GOD OF THE PIGEONS

The layout is practically the same. I don't need any stamps really but I go in anyway to see if Kevin's there. He is. I see him at once behind the new low-level counter, he's much greyer than he was before, unless it's the atmospheric lighting. His face has a slow fade-out-to-lost look which distresses me. I don't want to feel pity for the only real person I can talk to, I want to see he's doing okay.

'How you keeping, Angie?' he asks me.

'I'm alright,' I say. 'I've left school now, I was expelled for refusing to go to Assembly. They said I was an atheist. I said that was a matter for my reason and conscience. It was against the school rules to be an atheist they had the pleasure of informing me. 'Rules' are the only things they think about in that place. It's what you might call a mentally sterile environment. I'm so glad to get out of there.'

Kevin leans across to me, says without warning and in a voice of menace and aggression, 'Your free-thinking hero, on his deathbed, said he'd been wrong about everything. Didn't know that, did you. He said there was no morality without religion. None. On his deathbed! He cried and said he'd been wrong about every single thing. You hear that?' Kevin leans closer, I notice his breath is sharp and oniony and his eyeballs are a mass of squirmy spun-red fibres. 'You have to get in touch with Reality, Angie.'

His breath and eyes kind of mesmerise me for a moment and I notice that the questions I'd been saving up to talk about have all fled from my mind leaving me blank and empty. There seems to be no possibility of any more questions at all. I can't understand why Kevin is saying this stuff to me as though he thinks I think ideas are less important than personality. It was a mistake giving Kevin so much personal information. I can see that. Maybe he believes if an idol's crushed I'm crushed too. He does look angry and as if he'd like to crush me. But it must be he's just telling me to give up thinking about the questions we used to discuss. I'd been enthusiastic about the realisation morality wasn't dependent on religion around the time the post office closed down, I recalled, and it seemed Kevin'd remembered that. Or perhaps he's another one that

SEE YOU LATER, FRANÇOIS MARIE

thinks I'm bonkers. This thought makes me gulp a bit. I mean, s'posing he's right. But no, I fight it. Who is he to pronounce such a judgement? *Poor Kevin, he wants to wound me and he is wounding me. But not in the way he thinks he is.* I'm standing by the counter emptily, leaning on the corner for support. I'm dazed but I'm recovering. If there is no friend, there is none and I'll have to come to terms with it. And there's still François Marie, he'll be there forever if I want him to be, in his incorporeal way.

At work I'm the office junior along with Darren and Ben. Ben's into buffoonery, with a shallow personality. All up front, what you see is what you get, a laugh a minute, how exhausting. I don't even understand most of his jokes. His girlfriend's a trainee secretary at the office, a jealous type who's wary of me. She needn't be. I hate seeing the way their relationship operates, the manipulations and manoeuvres. She alternates between emotional battering and a breathtaking sequence of eyelash fluttering. He plays the clown. I find the whole routine sickening, a masquerading of trashy feminine and masculine stereotypes. Darren is musty-smelling and unsexy and available. I ask him if he thinks our political system is truly democratic and whether he believes in gods and goblins. I ask these things perfunctorily, not expecting any surprises, and guess what, there are none, he fobs me off without considering the questions. And yet he tries ceaselessly and energetically to interest me in him. Making sheep eyes at me, trying to get me on a date. No chance whatever. He has nothing going for him, he makes me puke. Darren and I, and sometimes Ben as well, have to make regular trips to the post office. The first couple of times we go Kevin isn't there.

It's a Thursday, late October. The three of us are going along there to get some books of stamps and send out a few packets and heavy duty parcels which we'll have to get weighed. I'm glad when I notice Kevin's here today. I wanted to see him and have the opportunity to detach myself from him once and for all and go into hiding. The faded-lost look he had on his face the last time I was in here is replaced by a hardened knowing expression which appals me.

'Angie,' he says in a false way which goes with his eyes, 'you're looking great.' To go with this statement he gives a kind of blokish wink at Darren and Ben. 'Glad to see you're alright now.'

I can't make out what he's talking about. 'Was I ill?'

'I used to be worried about you. All that stuff you used to go on about. You've turned out alright.' Another winkish gesture, this time involving a sideways movement of the whole head and directed solely at Darren. Maybe because Darren's standing close to me Kevin's got hold of the idea there might be something between us. Darren, if I could see his face, most likely has an expression which says there is.

'Great hairstyle, Angie.'

'Yes, I had it cut,' I tell him.

But waves of shock are passing over me at the extent of Kevin's betrayal. As I stand there feeling embarrassed by Kevin and for him I make the decision to leave the town for good by the end of the year. Then as soon as I can, I force myself to look the part Kevin's written in for me.

Apparently it was all a game to him before so I'll make quite sure he'll see nothing of me now. And I make a mental note I'll always make myself invisible to the creep Kevin and others like him. I do an awful simper, the kind Delia would be capable of, and make little appeasing movements, lowering with my head, as though to agree Kevin is right. *Once there was cause for worry but now I'm a normal girl.*

Because I'm not quite tough enough to brave it on my own though, I have to summon up the image of my secret and only friend. In no way do I deceive myself that he's really present, it goes without saying. That's the kind of fantasy I'm just not into. I know better than anybody François Marie doesn't really exist in the here and now, but pretending he's there gives me strength. It's making me puke standing here simpering in front of Kevin and Co.. There are quite a lot of parcels to see to and I just know we'll be here for some time. To help me keep the game going as long as it'll take, and hold my spirits up till I get out on the

SEE YOU LATER, FRANÇOIS MARIE

pavement, breathe the cleaner air, I whisper as quietly as I can, 'See you later, outside the post office, François Marie.' And it suddenly hits me that having François Marie is probably a lot like having the god experience, and I also remind myself that very soon now and with no looking back whatsoever attached to it, I'll be out of here for good.

ENTERTAINING ANGIE

A NGIE TAKES AWAY THE plates, looks out across the burger bar tables. Nothing about much, except there's this one guy. She notices him because of his funny lip. The lip is crooked, pushing down towards the left side of his chin. Seeing him from the right briefly and in passing it looks as though he might not have a mouth. She laughs, puts the plates on the counter and saunters back to the tables. The guy notices back, smiles crookedly, she twiddles the pepper pots on the tables, getting closer. There's something she likes, an irony in the eyes as though he's seeing through a lot of falseness. His eyes are grey and sharp, amused but not bitter. Well, maybe bitter, it's not a thing she'd mind if there's wit present. He looks as if he has wit. The crooked mouth is pleasing. It will not, it cannot, compromise and pretend to be as other mouths are, most mouths. And there's this thing about him that says having this crooked mouth as well as looking at the world in an ironic way, are choices he's personally made.

Next day he's back with two other guys. They're ordering coffees and he's sweeping back his straight fair hair. But not in a way that annoys her, in a way that looks abstracted, as though he's having real thoughts about something else, entertaining an interesting idea. Not pretentious, not self-conscious. Today, with the friends here, he's all laughter; sardonic and cross-questioning. Angie can't hear what's said but she knows by instinct from his look he's aware that he and she are two of a kind, experiencing similar critical insights, and that he has not held her ordinary symmetrical lips against her in any way. She likes the fact he hasn't been taken in by appearance. 'Hi,' he says, and 'Hi,' they both say, separating themselves off at once from the other two at the table. A world apart, world of their own. The other guys look understanding, look somewhere else. In this way Angie and Dave become at once *an item*.

ENTERTAINING ANGIE

Personal recognition reinforced by social. Dave has a froth mark of coffee on the crooked lip. Even this does not reduce him. He's in control, or he doesn't care. She is easy, more than happy with this. They meet and go for drinks and go to the cinema several times. In the near dark she sees him with that knowing smile of his as if he's seeing layers beneath the surface of things, privately asking relevant questions. And that laugh he has, it's not about trite worldly stuff, about not missing a trick, some superficial thing like how he's done this certain guy down and so feels cosily and mindlessly *the best*, like some of the guys she knows. He hasn't taken a sharpie short cut, been streetwise in any way. Hasn't made any false assumption that these things would be of value. She feels that. The thing he knows, that she reads in his face, is something about the way things *are*. He's seen beneath what's proposed; what's happening at some empty level, all around them. He is someone who questions things. She's proud of him, not that she means exactly *pride*, and it's not hero worship. He's a philosopher, just as she herself is. There's something about his face, something. Oh, doesn't he look just a little bit like Voltaire? But more than just a bit, excepting the mouth he's completely the living image. That sparkling cadaverous and ironic expression. Maybe she herself doesn't have it, which is probably the reason nobody's discovered those qualities are entirely what she is inside. But now, to have been seen and understood for once, feels wonderful.

Here they are together in the half-dark cinema. They haven't kissed yet. Is it because he's afraid he mightn't quite get to her mouth at the right angle, making a kiss an awkward thing? Maybe he's afraid that she's afraid he'll try, and go brushing at her face with those difficult lips of his, missing. And so, if she should go and start kissing *him*? Well, it wouldn't be that easy because she happens to be sitting on his right side, she can hardly see he has a mouth at all from here. And he's staring hard at the screen, come to think of it, furiously hard, as if the film is quite important. It has seemed like a fairly silly film so far, but maybe there's a subtext, she thinks perhaps there must be. But there's this bit of anxiety in her about whether or not he likes her, especially as when they part no further date is made. And then the next day, a Saturday, he comes in the burger bar where she's waitressing. Where it's quite busy being the weekend, where there's a smell of fries and fattiness, and beans and re-heated pie. He says will she, would she. It's all casual and that, but will she would she. He says about visiting these mates of his. Friends, they are, close friends. Sunday, yes tomorrow, it'd be nice and that. Then will she, would she. Oh the joy of it, he's inviting her into his intimate world, she's that flattered. So Sunday she meets him, he's waiting for her at the corner of her street, his smile at its height. *Would you say then Dave, in the world as you've observed it, 'That everything necessarily exists in view of the best possible end'?*

At the house of these friends it's anything but casual. They're horribly prepared with stiff and smiling ceremony. Angie is surprised, what have they been told? She's also surprised because these friends are a married couple with a baby. Jake and Doreen and little Dee. She'd thought they'd be all singles, sitting around, that maybe they'd talk about the meaning of truth or what it means to say God exists, a relaxed thing but with the sort of tension she likes to be part of, happening. *Talk.*

Instead there's this over-polite show with the couple-friends doing this kind of smiling dance to one another as if to demonstrate what good partners they are, and the baby dribbling and gurgling all the while. Which is fine, which is fine, but they keep holding it out as if to be admired. As if to be admired by Angie! It's that she finds quite hard to take. Nothing is said at all, or what *Angie* thinks of as nothing, and the baby is put into the space between them as if that will be enough to please her. *Entertaining Angie.* She looks at Dave but he's lost on some weird trip, making these googlie noises and waggling all his fingers. As if he's lost his reason, he's lost his thinking mind. So is this where he hangs out then? She can't believe it, it's like being at home with her parents. And there's a funny atmosphere as if they think she thinks how wonderful it would be to be like them, and maybe if she and Dave . . . And as Dave has invited her here and she herself has actually come here with him then it might be a likely thing to suppose that . . . From their point of view, that . . . She's shocked at the thought that they might think, no that they most definitely *are* thinking right now—That she and he, and isn't she the lucky one. She's unable to finish any one of these sentences though she's read through the full horror of their conclusions. Uneasily, she sits on one of the matching turquoise armchairs deciding she hates Sunday afternoons, she'll never be able to see one normally again. She's got to get out of here but she's too polite to just stand up and leave. Meanwhile the display goes on. The kid is held closer and closer to her, no doubt to bring out her motherly desire. They're probably getting desperate because she hasn't given the correct responses. But though she can't get up and go, she can't join in either. So she sits aghast and silent hardly managing a smile. She's wondering about Dave in all of this. All she can see and hear of him now is this googling and gaggling, He's doing the big-daddy thing, and trying to make sure she's taking it in. The whole thing is a colossal pain. She sees him watching her out of the corner of his eye, like she should be impressed or something. The kid screams, well who wouldn't, and starts straining and going red. The parents chuckle and Doreen, the mother (Angie won't even think the word *Mum*) takes it off at last, for changing. Angie reflects. It's not that she hates the kid, it's that she doesn't want this to be *her* world. But she's embarrassed and hurt to think that this is the thing they've put on the cards for her. Nobody here knows her, even Dave. Why should they imagine she'd want this? It makes her angry to think they'd dare to make such an assumption. That they *have* made it is in their every gesture. And then Dave's getting up to go and get beers. This is the end, she's not even a beer drinker. Sunday afternoon and beers. It makes her feel ill. And when he's gone, kind of waltzed smugly through the door, Jake and Doreen—Doreen's back with the kid and a bib and baby food—they kind of take her to one side, and make these stupid faces and significant eyes at her. They keep saying stuff like, 'Oh he's a wonderful guy is Dave. Never mind some of the funny things he says, he's a lovely guy, Dave is.' And Angie definitely gets the feeling

GOD OF THE PIGEONS

they're trying to compensate for Dave's crooked lip by going over the top about his virtue. *Virtue according to them*, that is. And when he comes back in with the six-packs, there's this cheesy knowing look passing round between the three of them and she sees it was all set up for her to be with them and they'd put in a word. She's sick with rage at being so mistaken, and there's another horror she has to face. She comes to understand, while sitting here, that Dave's little bit of irony, the *funny things*, are also just compensation for the lip. He doesn't see the world in any interesting way, he doesn't see anything at all. It grieves her to think it, but she suddenly sees quite clearly that it's so. He'd drop everything *funny* if he was offered normality on a plate, he'd cut off the lip if he could and have an ordinary one. That smile of his which seems to show there's some wit to him is no more than a façade. She waits while they drink, trying to join in here and there out of pity for their misunderstanding, a bit of a smirk in her realising her *own* misunderstanding was as great as theirs.

When at last they leave it's mid-evening, a lovely faded look, and she strolls down the road with Dave, just glad to get away from Jake and Doreen still winking and blinking on the doorstep, waving fixedly till they're out of sight. In her mortified heart she doubts she'll ever be able to speak to Dave again. There's just one last thing she wants to put to him, but he looks so far off in the contemplation of future pleasantness she believes that he will not hear her. 'Do you think, Dave?' she finally manages to ask him, 'would you be of the opinion at all, that *there is no effect without a cause*?'

MY SECRET ROLLERSKATES

Woman in a red jacket, black ski pants. Her hair's poked into a scarf but it's sticking out in spikes. Eyes, brown with flecks of yellow, uneasy tigerish. She's hunching forward to drink from her paper cup, flat gold earrings swaying in towards the corners of her mouth. These are the instant details Anneke sees.

The two women sit on navy blue plastic café chairs, eyes far off, watching the slow undulations of the Zuiderzee. Then they're both looking closer in, at the line of swans bobbing on the mini waves like bath toys. It's choppy next to the wall, rows of curtailed wavelets all brought together in a bunch. Chunky bits of foam detach themselves, fly up in the air. The swans stare back at the women with frowning concentration, beaks orange and intent, the whole flotilla rocking. Then all at once the swans lose interest. They've suddenly noticed the raised and then lowered arm of a bread-thrower further along the wall. With a quick about turn they're moving off in that direction.

Isn't that a tear Anneke can see edging down the pale rather long face next to her? Maybe not, could've been shifting light from the window. But yes, it is a tear, though dabbed away fast with a corner of the red sleeve, a quick-flick gesture which can't quite be seen. In the eye visible to her, the left eye, she sees another tear starting. Anneke herself is feeling fragile, her mind's in a flurry and it's as though the tears are being shed for both of them, freeing her from the need to express grief. And then the woman's speaking, her voice distant and soft. 'The Zuiderzee always has this way of making me feel it's myself I'm looking at.'

Anneke wants to say something back.

Roll and splash of slight waves. Anneke and Sofie sitting side by side with paper coffee cups, looking out. They've started to talk. Sofie's received a tissue, Anneke, the information that what's wrong with Sofie is uncertainty. She's just about to get married but is having serious second thoughts. 'Which is nothing new with me,' Sofie admits. Anneke tells Sofie about her unsatisfactory marriage, how she's wanted to get out for a long time but has never found the right kind of courage. Until today. All the morning she'd thought about leaving Hans—leaving him for good. Unbelievable that she's packed a small bag, mentally composed a note for him, driven away from Harlingen, got this far. Right now she's feeling strange and cut loose.

The two of them feel this ease together, as strangers can when there's a mutual interest but no real involvement. It's comforting, telling things about where they live, what their lives are like. Sofie's from Amsterdam and her wedding's fixed for the weekend. But she had this urge to get away, is driving up to Friesland, and though she can't quite see everything clearly, there's this feeling she mightn't go back. As Sofie speaks, her eyes flutter and wince, roam across surfaces, remain unsettled. She hardly seems to alight anywhere. And there's this hovering quality about her body as though she'd rather be flying. The head of spiky yellow hair rises and falls bird-like, the gold earrings glimmer, cast shadows on her face. Anneke talks about Hans, how their life together is quiet, how she doesn't mind that, *and yet* . . . 'I don't *hate* that life but it doesn't seem good enough, or, it doesn't seem the right life. There has to be a time when you can turn round and say *no* to something.' Her voice lifts because of the scariness of the thought that you may never do this turning, that you may just carry on and on. 'This morning I left Hans.' Anneke bangs the light paper cup down on the table top and goes silent. Already, she's begun to have her doubts. Because isn't everything in this life just as flawed? 'I really left him, but . . .' They both look out at the water.

'Ideally, what I'd like is to get back into education,' Sofie says. 'Where I left off. Archaeology, that's what I love. I wish I'd seen it through before, but I gave up the course. Maybe now's the time.' Suddenly she waves her arms. 'The idea of the remote past being right here all around, and us

MY SECRET ROLLERSKATES

looking for clues and finding little bits of it. You piece things together. You know.'

It's a moment of dream sharing.

'It'd be so great to travel, I've hardly been anywhere. Hans is such a stay-at-home. Being on my own could turn out to be fantastic. There are so many places I really want to go, right now I'm headed for Amsterdam. No, I'd be crazy going back to Hans, and I've left haven't I, I've already made the break, packed and everything. If I go back now I'll only have to go through the same thing again, or stay forever, I mean. I expect the first night's the worst, I just have to get through that. It must be possible to move on.'

Sofie and Anneke walking in the wind along the length of the Afsluitdijk, Anneke holding her hair down, or trying to, Sofie's spikes defying the headscarf. And the wind animates both of them, gives them a distinct sense of *now*.

'It's amazing, I've been able to leave, to look for a new life. Just like that.'

Sofie agrees, with an expansive high swinging of her arms. Between the IJsselmeer and the Waddensee she describes invisible arcs. Then she goes on to talk about her own relationship, having to speak as loud as she can, just to be heard above the wind. 'Martijn's in complete denial about the past, just dreads being reminded there is one. To me that's sad. He doesn't want to know anything about say, the history of the human race. He wants to live in a sealed-off little vacuum and pretend things have always been the same. And why? It's because he's afraid of change, basically that. He can't face up to the idea that one day he himself won't be here. How can I end up with a man like this? *End up.* That phrase alone is enough to drive me wild.'

Sofie and Anneke laugh together then Sofie turns serious.

'Me, it's different for me, I sort of think I'll be *in* things, maybe that sounds mad. What I mean is, bits of me will be around in artifacts, say in shards of old china that were cups or plates I'd used, in the remains of buildings where I might have sat, say the library, anywhere where I've been with my feelings, in things I once valued even if they're broken up now. Martijn calls that kind of idea empty sentiment. But what it means is I don't have to worry about the now so much, because in a way I'm already safe in the future if you see what I mean, even though it hasn't happened yet. It leaves me free to be changeable. Martijn calls history my escape route. I sometimes wonder Anneke, why he wants to marry me at all. My worst times are when I get to thinking he really wants to annihilate me, to wrap me up in a life where no more changes are possible. I do have a problem with that, I can tell you.'

'When I first got married to Hans I was so happy. It was the ultimate, the perfect dream. I came down from that, of course it's inevitable, no one's to blame. But the picnics, they played their part, without them I might have felt better about things.'

'Picnics?' Sofie asks her.

'Hans and me, we used to go on picnics when we were first together. To start with I thought, how romantic. But it didn't work, it just brought out the fundamental differences between us. He's easy going is Hans and doesn't like squandering energy on what's not important—his way of looking at things, not mine, by the way. So, with the picnics he just wanted to put down any old where, by the side of the road, could be at the wall next to the beach loos for all he cared. I mean it. I said, "Call this a picnic?" I couldn't stand it, making our little encampment in some ugly place, somewhere without a view. What was the point? Well, there was this time, I kept on making him move with me to a better spot. But you know, he was unaware, unaware! Just tagged along with me, all unwilling, sighing and rolling his eyes to the sky. And this undermined me I think, and it didn't feel good anywhere we tried. So we kept on moving all the afternoon looking for somewhere better, the perfect picnic spot. Perhaps you think it's nutty, but for me it was the beginning of the end. Yet you know, and this frightens me, in a way Hans was right.'

Sofie nods. 'He thinks one thing's just as good as another.'

MY SECRET ROLLERSKATES

'Sort of. But it's a matter of feeling, isn't it. Hans and me, we see things differently.'

Sofie's sympathetic. 'Basic incompatibility, it is really. Same as with me and Martijn. For instance, Martijn can't have his deeper self touched at all, there must be no shadows, no echoes, it's all part of his anxiety. It would be my life's task to keep him comfortably on the surface, make sure things were bland so's he wouldn't be ruffled. Of course talking about him like this makes him sound worse than he is. He has some great qualities, he's a good person. But, as you see, we're hardly on the same rowboat.'

'It would be nothing to spend whole hours standing in the kitchen with my arms soaking in a bowl of washing-up water, say, imagining myself miles away. And then I'd think, "But how will I get there?" The same process every day, at the end of it the same stumbling block. Until this morning. This morning I fantasised about having this pair of rollerskates. They were right there in my kitchen, leaning against one corner. I saw myself sail out of the window on them, glide across the lawn—don't laugh—the street, then Harlingen. They rolled me forward and away, whizzing me along over every kind of surface. Flashy skates, silver and black, that'd take me anywhere, take me away from my grossly imperfect life. How sad is that? My secret rollerskates.' Anneke's stopped walking, she stares at the regular grey and white waves. Below them a line of chopped-up foam, swans at the water's edge.

'On the one hand it's tempting to think of settling, there again it wouldn't be right for me. At this moment I too am being pulled in the direction of change. We seem to be moving along parallel lines. I know I'm missing out on some important things but I can't help feeling that with Martijn it'll be the end of the line, and my real life will be over. Hard but . . . this is where my idea of history comes in, it's always there for me. I never have to feel I'm just hopelessly lost, because somehow what it boils down to is, I belong to everywhere.'

The two women stare out at the swans on those mini-sized waves.

GOD OF THE PIGEONS

'This thing about looking for perfection can make it really hard to do anything in the real world. You can get so inhibited by the thought you'll never find it, and what you'll come upon is so much less, that in the end you just can't move for fear. And then, the rollerskates, wow!' Anneke delves into her bag and brings out a dryish bread roll which she tears in half. Then she and Sofie stand by the water throwing small pinched off morsels to the swans, laughing at the way every last swan in the line is zooming toward them, correctly reading the meaning of their thrown out arms. They make the bits smaller so it will go further, make more swans happy, just for one second's swallowing before the anxiety floods back. When the bread is finished they turn towards the café, trying not to see the still waiting faces with their criss-crossed intensity. The wind's so high now it just pushes them along.

'It's so strange here,' Sofie says. 'Well, *I* feel strange. The way the water ends up like that by the wall. A lake doesn't end that way, a lake has its own natural ending. This is a cut-off sea and it will never let you forget that. I get this terrible painful feeling just thinking of it. The Zuiderzee. It can never arrive anywhere, can it.'

Both of them laugh yet feel sad.

'But I'm sort of comfortable here as well,' Sofie goes on. 'A real sea would be filling me with tension because it would be pushing me to some finality, there'd be that pressure. I'd be feeling I must do this, or I must do that, it would be utterly infuriating. But not this poor little Zuiderzee, no. It's a nowhere place this, neither sea nor lake, and it looks angry, don't you think. What a flurry of cut off waves. It does remind me of how I feel about my life but it doesn't try to persuade me that I should be other than I am. I love it for that, d'you see what I mean?'

'Yes, I do.' Anneke's voice has gone quiet with thought. 'But this wind, it's becoming impossible, let's go and get another coffee.'

As they walk back she tells Sofie, 'Everyone has their personal Zuiderzee response, don't they, this feeling there's a message for them, for their own lives. As for me, I've an idea I feel much more uneasy here than you, I really sort of experience the frustration, I mean the sight of

MY SECRET ROLLERSKATES

the cut-off sea.' She shudders. 'And I'm obsessed with the idea that it's lost its salt. For me, that's the worst thought. The Zuiderzee can never be anything but a failure, in its own terms I mean, of course. Its role is one of sacrifice for the general good. A sacrificial sea. I get a sense of claustrophobia, of perpetual discontent. And it makes me feel, shit, I've gotta take action *now*.' They stand together, still for a while in the now too-sharp wind, see the line of swans far off, shifting in the direction of a new bread thrower.

'And at the same time it's saying to me there's no reason to even try,' Anneke says savagely, the wind carrying her voice in jolts away somewhere so that Sofie can't really hear her. 'At this moment I feel as hopeless as I ever did, in spite of my newly-found conviction. Oh, maybe I've lost the will to act after all, Sofie. What's happened is the image of my rollerskates has been getting fainter and fainter while we've been standing here talking. Now it's gone altogether. Coming to this place was definitely a mistake for me.'

Sofie catches the tail end of what Anneke's saying, looks dejected, then shakes her head. 'I've got a feeling you'll find your fantasy skates. Don't despair. Who knows, maybe they're waiting for you, they could be anywhere, even in that little cut off sea. Yeah, you'll find them. Just when you need them they'll turn up.'

They smile together at Sofie's way of putting things, lean forward on their toes, look out across the stretch of water.

'When that time comes you'll stop being inhibited by the fear you'll never find perfection so why try to do anything. You'll take your chance.'

'You know, really, I've gone beyond that. I've come to see there's no such thing as perfection. Not in the real world. Perfection is only an idea, a beautiful idea but it can't translate outside itself. It's not something you can look for, not a thing you can live with. It's a kind of myth. It's human to want it maybe, but it's not human to have it. And suppose you could find it, just suppose. Well, you wouldn't be able to stand it. It's not possible to live that way. You know, there can never *be* perfection. Because if you had that you'd need to get away from it. Once you've seen this you ask yourself, what's the point in trying to change anything? It's why, deep down, I know I'm always doomed, always thinking of leaving Hans, but not really feeling there's good enough reason to go ahead with it.'

'Unless . . .' says Sofie. 'Unless change for change's sake is the natural human state. And the idea of perfection is just the vehicle for moving yourself on.'

'Well, it seems to me everything's paradoxical. I mean, we want to arrive at the perfect thing and we want to stay there. Yet we couldn't stand it. And we want change and movement and yet we can't stand that either. We're constantly shifting from the one idea to the other, never really satisfied . So still what's the point in leaving Hans?'

'Well, maybe there is none. And *yet* . . .'

'Yes, that's us isn't it. That's the word for us alright. '*Yet*.'

'The rollerskates are the *yet* in my life. There they are in the corner, shiny with possibility. I might skate away on them or concede they're a fantasy and just leave them where I can keep an eye on them.'

'Maybe it's the fantasies themselves that are the important thing,' Sofie says. 'Your rollerskates are working for you, aren't they, letting you develop in the direction you need to go. My idea of history's the same thing, giving me the courage to carry on being myself.'

Anneke carries the image through. 'And I'll skate off into the future, across the land, across the Zuiderzee, recognising no boundaries? Even if I never move from exactly where I'm standing now, all life's textures will be negotiable?'

'Something tells me you really will.

CLOUDING THE LIGHT

THE MAGICIAN IS TEARING up paper. It's falling to the floor in shreds, what will happen? There can be no way things will be alright, the paper is in shreds forever now, no hope of getting back to being just a newspaper, the way it was before. And yet everybody knows this will happen, the newspaper will be repaired. The audience knows but doesn't know how. Jon knows too. He sits out there in the auditorium with his mum and dad.

Is what he remembers vaguely, he's not sure what age he'd have been. But it was before his mother had the car accident, so seven or eight. What he remembers strongly is how fear darted up inside him in steely points, yet he had this calm certain knowledge underneath that the magician was in control and, even though it didn't seem possible he'd make everything come back to normal by the end of the trick, all would be well.

So no need for fear, but still he can hardly breathe. Just this one narrow strip of paper left. Everyone's quiet now, waiting to see if the magician has taken himself into some blind alley from which there's no escape, no coming back. It's dark everywhere except for the bright circle of light in which the magician smiles, lifts up his hands, flings away all of the strips of paper except one. And then he's turning his back on the audience, he's picking up the torn paper, folding it away somewhere; into his pocket, *somewhere*, but who really cares, it's trash, it's waste to be thrown out. A sad story then, the magician's a failure. Reason kicks in. Of course, it was impossible, the magician was only kidding them and they fell for it. A half-sigh passes through the watching crowd. They're holding breath, just a bit of it lets out. And then the magician's back into fast action, he's holding up his hands. What's happening, oh what is happening? There's a sound started up, drums, the throbbing roll of drums. Getting louder. A smile on the magician's face which draws Jon in. And then *wowee*, the hands are flung up and apart and there's the newspaper, that one last strip and all the other discarded bits put back together, all one. The audience gasps and Jon gasps too.

Destruction and restoration.

Is what he says to himself now he's older, now he is a magician too. Wondering if this was the time when he'd been hooked and hammered to the craft of wizardry. The thought of the power, thought of the bringing back from the jaws of death. Lazarus. Is that what did it, was that the moment? Looking up into that circle of white light. Face of the magician, smiling. The raised hands. All eyes on the hands. And the paper flapping out as one, all the bits back to how they were. A miracle. *Before your very eyes*. Jon looking out of the window. A nearly empty scene, just the one or two people in sight. Only a few weeks ago it was full summer, height of the season. And now this. Endings. Endings for him, especially. Jon lights up a cigarette; makes an unsuccessful attempt to get away from what's on his mind. Louise is still in bed, she calls him over.

Which stops him from staring out at the pool beyond the chalet window for traces of fuzziness—the evidence that his vision is drastically worse than it was yesterday. This is always the subject of his thoughts, somewhere in the background even if not admitted to: his oncoming blindness, looking for signs of it his everyday occupation now. He has just closed his left eye to see how much is visible through his good right eye on its own, he does this several times a day. Louise will have noticed what he's doing, she's looking at him with a mild reproach. Jon goes over and sits on the side of the bed. Now she's all bright smiles as though to deny his terrors or to chase them away. He crushes the cigarette into an ashtray, gets into bed and falls on and into Louise's waiting body. He wishes it was passion she was offering him instead of sympathy, an escape route to somewhere sweeter than his own bleak thoughts. But he's well aware they haven't been in love with one another for years. Her kindness wounds him.

CLOUDING THE LIGHT

Because he has known for several months now that his eyes are failing him. *He really will be blind.* He says these words silently again and again, trying to get used to the idea, closing his eyes to picture darkness. And he won't let himself open them again, fights back the desire to blink. Tells himself he needs to experience what it will be like to not have the choice, wanting to be ready for a world in which whether his eyes are open or shut, whether he blinks or not, the dark will be there. There will be no formula of words, no special incantations, *Abracadabra*, to change things back again. This booking at the Sombolito Holiday Park in Tenerife is his last. The season's over now, just one more performance tonight then home to Maidstone. He's up and making coffee, Louise is in the shower. Looking out again he sees the deserted pool. A splatter of dry eucalyptus leaves on turquoise water. He guesses the details, their reality is just a blur.

And thinks about the past. Recalls how the magician had lived in the same street as his granddad. Jon was staying with his grandparents around the time he was nine years' old. It was after the accident. Jon's mother, wheelchair-bound, had been unable to cope. He had wished so much he had a wizard's hands so he could change all this and have her walking again. Dreamed himself waving a magician's wand and saying secret words, saw his mother getting up from the wheelchair and stepping towards him, he Jon, making it happen, succeeding where all the doctors had failed. Miraculous. Going to the house of the magician with other kids in the street.

Where he seemed ordinary and disappointing. Wearing long jumpers, rumpled and uneven, frayed at the wrist, his trousers baggy around the knees, his hair grizzly-grey. But there was this distracted look about him as though his mind was somewhere else and this at least was encouraging. Jon expected his magician to be set apart from the everyday. So perhaps it didn't matter so much what the man looked like, Jon came to feel, as long as he was up above the world somehow, unconnected and free. Jon looked at the sky, picturing the magician there, wanting him there. He imagined the man sailing past the window on a cloud, a confusion in his mind between the magic of miracles and professional sleight of hand. The last thing he would have ever wanted was to sort out this confusion once and for all. Same now as then.

Is what he suddenly realises, despite the knowledge he now has. On his way to the rehearsal, walking past the pool, concentrating his eyes. Yes, the leaves are there, yes eucalyptus. Here's the tree near the water's edge. Amazingly tall that tree, the trunk ridged and riveted—he runs his hand across its bark in passing. Sense of defiance. Feels a comfort in touch much more now that he's going blind, plus a bit of anger at the pride of place sight has among the senses, as though to say, by losing that you'd be losing everything. Looks back at the tree, already a hazy darkness against grey-blue. Hard to believe this might be his last public performance. And it doesn't have to be, he could go for more bookings. Saying all this to himself as he walks along the path to the hall where the show will happen. He is the show, he will *make* it happen. He must! But the will in the words makes him sense a background doubt, as if he'll shock himself and cancel. *No*, he says out loud, and hearing it disturbs him even more. Does he need to be convinced so much?

And he takes himself back to the kitchen of the magician. All the kids in the street had somehow got themselves crammed into that compact space. It was trick-afternoon, or morning, he can't remember when. But there were the kids, some who weren't friendly to him, or to anybody; lone kids and unknown kids. All there and equal. The ones that might lie in wait for you on the way home from school and beat you up for fun, the stuck-up ones who knew all the maths in class. Didn't matter here, in the magician's kitchen. They were all friendly together, all innocent together. Their eyes passed from sink to draining board to shelf, following the movement of the magician's hands. All easy together in this equality, all friends now, here, in this unmagical setting, that still, in spite of appearances, was taking them out of the ordinary world and into somewhere special. Or *up to*. Because it always felt as though it was the sky you were heading for at such moments. Sky, not earth. Looking out of the uncurtained kitchen window and seeing sun. Then glancing down

CLOUDING THE LIGHT

to the street and staring at this tiny seated figure struggling along on the pavement, her shadow seeming to pass the window clouding the light. He wants to look away but can't. Sees his mother below going along jerkily in the wheelchair to his grandparents', her hands gripping and pushing, propelling herself forward. Can't see the hands but imagines them, imagines her frailty and the tension in her shoulders, the sweat breaking out on her lip. Jon, as a boy, clenching his hands against the rim of the sink. In his mind he's stripping his mother of all the awful things, her wheelchair and that look of pain; throwing all of it away like waste paper. What's left is his mother as she used to be. There she is, held together as if by magic, inside all these layers of badness that have somehow covered her up. The hidden indestructible mother. He, only he, has the power to release her from all of this. He's pressing his eyes shut, forming a picture of his mother walking, or running. Or flying. Beautiful illusion.

Which remains with him for a minute here on this stage in the Tenerife end-of-season afternoon as he prepares for the hoops and tricycle trick which leads into the finale. It's one of his favourites, a tricksy trick, large and visible and strongly silver. A beauty at its best. He's standing facing the space where the audience will be later on and he keeps on missing with the hoops. His eyes at the corners are nearly empty of sight. Shadowy dark triangles get in the way. He tries blinking sharply through to brightness but it isn't quite working. At the moment of the blink things are clearer, but it doesn't last. He's squinting, his line of vision is uneven, it wobbles and bounds. His eyes are out of control. He hears the clang of a metal hoop as it bounces past him, hits the stage floor, goes sideways, clatters. And right there where the audience will be Louise is standing, looking anxious but biting it back. Putting on that brave face that so unnerves him.

Is how he pictures it. She doesn't want him to be aware of any of his mistakes. Louise catching the falling hoops with her eyes. Her eyes scoop up the failures, hurry them away. Just as she will be waiting to catch him too, if *he* should fall. The ground is below, he can see it coming up. Louise won't let him reach it, would never let him get that far. She is a basket woven with threads of safety, all for him. She'll swoop down and scoop him up even if he wasn't falling anyway. He knows what falling is, though she wouldn't like him to. And Jon feels angry suddenly, resenting her protective softness, her deception. He's a magician after all, he knows when there's an illusion being offered him. He hears in his ears already, what she'll say, 'Darling, it's fine. It's okay.' Her kindly-meant rescue-party of words, her ability to change the subject to neutral territory. When he says something like, 'I know I'm going to miss the next one,' she'll downcast her eyes discreetly, letting him move on to a stronger way of thinking unobserved. This is the way she'll guide his thoughts. And she won't look up again till he's reached the next haven. *Safety net.*

Seeing himself back in the magician's kitchen and looking out at sky. Which is white and blue and never still as it moves from one side of the window to the other. Jon as a boy, having to stand right on tiptoe to see what the clouds become. Cloud faces, cloud figures, amazing cloud palaces and islands in a stream. Clouds passing and changing. He can't see to the end of them, no matter how far he stretches. A shadow's moving below on the pavement, but Jon's determined not to look. In case it's his mother, and he, only nine years' old, and not knowing how to bring the power back to her legs again. Over at the sink the magician balances an egg on a bubble-blowing frame, holds a glass of water upside down on a beermat, nothing spilling, meanwhile the egg has vanished. Finds a coin in some boy's pocket causing laughter, the egg comes back on a ledge near the ceiling, next it turns into a plastic mouse. But was it a proper egg anyway, to start with? All the kids are in doubts, jeers starting up. Then there's the egg again, in the magician's right hand. He taps it with his wand, it breaks. Albumen and yolk trail to the draining-board. No more laughter, the egg is real. Jon wants to reach out and touch the broken eggshell but somehow his arm won't move. Instead, he thinks, when I'm grown up, I'll be a magician too.

CLOUDING THE LIGHT

As he now is. It's evening showtime, he in his night-suited mode; Louise the magician's assistant, a flourish of sequins and fishnets. Mermaid-like, she swishes and twirls. The magician bows to the small mustered end-of-season crowd. Can this really be his last show ever? Standing up here on the small stage Jon thinks this question quickly, then disposes of it. A question too unthinkable to be asked. He's amazed the audience already with his hoop and bicycle trick. They're all keen now, all watching Jon, watching his hands. Some call out for the trick to be repeated. He laughs, acting as if he might *just* do the trick again. He has them all waiting. Waiting and watching. Truth is, he won't do the trick again. The magician determines everything, the magician never does an encore; this is the art of the unexpected. He picks up a newspaper which lies innocuously on an ornamental table. Louise in her swishing and twirling, extends her hand to him, brings out the clapping from the audience, draws all eyes to the magician at centre stage. 'And now . . ,' he calls out to them. 'Now I'm going to perform the World's Most Famous Paper Trick. What I'm going to do, Ladies and Gentlemen, Boys and Girls, is make the impossible happen. I'm going to tear up this ordinary newspaper which you see before you into tiny shreds, and then, I'm going to put it back together again. It doesn't always work though. I need your help, I need your powers of concentration.' He holds up the newspaper to the audience, gives a dazzling smile, opens one page after another to show them it's only a newspaper. They all stare, believing, yet disbelieving, wanting to see how he does it, not wanting to. Wanting the trick to work, wanting him to fail. Will he, won't he? He begins to tear off strips which he flings round him, showing they're finished, are of no more importance. More and more strips fall, until there's just the one left in his hands. Inconsequentially, he begins to gather up all the discarded pieces. Important to get every last one of them out of sight. As he finishes, the drums at front of stage begin to roll. The traditional thing. 'So, Ladies and Gentlemen, Boys and Girls.' He's smiling at the crowd, making them wait, filling up these few minutes with words. But his hands, his magician's hands have already started. At the centre of the remaining bit of paper he's holding up is a square of wire into which is folded a second newspaper identical to the destroyed one. As he talks he's easing this wire frame with his thumb, easing and easing it so that when the moment comes, after all the talking and the roll of drums, he will shake out the newspaper. *Hey Presto!*

Re-created.

The show now over, Louise still watches him with anxiety. He can't see her expression but there's a tension which he picks up on.

'Stop looking at me like that,' he says, angrily because he can't quite see how she *is* looking, his eyes that have let him down tightly drawn together into two aching slits. Trying to focus.

'Jon', Louise says but he won't stay to listen, he's got to get out of the chalet, go for a long night walk. He doesn't ask her if she wants to come too. She never walks, and he's happy about that, he likes being alone. Some of the time he does. He knows she's afraid for him and it makes him bitter.

As he goes by the pool in darkness. The performance went well, only one or two slips, easily incorporated. It works, having a few mini-disasters on the way to the final perfection. The audience doesn't believe the slips weren't intended anyway, or it's another case of they don't and they do. That's the thing with magic, all reactions are mixed from the word go. Yes and No, is and isn't. It will be, it never was. Nobody knows where they are, that's the best of it. That, when it all comes down to it, is what makes the thing work. The audience never knows what to think, never knows what the magician is going to do next, and when he's done it they never know *how* he did. Jon's still in love with conjuring. Conjuring something out of nothing, conjuring up everything that was least thought to be about to happen. The end of the show, the finale, is like a bow tied around all of the questions. The audience just has to let go and enter the spirit of the thing, they have to stop looking for answers. The magician brings everyone closer to early childhood.

CLOUDING THE LIGHT

Is how he puts it to himself, walking alone at night, trying to sort things out in his mind and look at where he's going in life. He's thinking right now about his relationship, not sure he's feeling so good about it any more. Louise is a wonderful woman, he won't deny it, he knows it's himself he's really unhappy with. Just himself. Given that fact, whatever Louise does or doesn't do is bound to jar. He understands this but it doesn't change anything, his mind is clouded over with self-contempt; he asks himself if he wants to separate. There's a long pause for him after he's raised the question, after which, a sigh. Thinking of the two of them in his small flat on the outskirts of Maidstone, seeing himself as a blindman, a man walking with the aid of a white stick.

While he stops by the side of the pool, looks over the low stone parapet and pictures the sea. He can hear the splash of waves; thinks of throwing himself into them. Then he walks on. A thought isn't quite so close as a feeling, he tells himself. He's not in danger. It's just one idea among many possibilities and needn't prove a necessity. Turning back towards the pool he makes out a moving shape near the eucalyptus tree, the white oval of a face. Louise? Next minute Louise is with him, her breathing has a wet strangled sound. He reaches out and touches her face, feels tears trickle across his hand. She leans her head against his chest and he kisses the top of it. There's a shampoo smell which he finds very childlike, he feels protective and sad. Puts out his hand into darkness, making a little grab at the air, says, 'Look, a falling star.' Then, 'It's all alright', he tells her.

Smiling at the power a magic word has to release someone from sorrow, because if you're down enough you're happy to settle for appearance, the clear gloss sheen of it.

'Is it really alright? Louise asks him nervously. Between *us*, I mean?'

After a while he says, 'Yes, it's alright between us. It'll be fine. I love you', recognising he's offering the very kind of comfort Louise offers *him*. Well, they're a pair of illusionists, after all, when you come right down to it. Some things he guesses never change.

RIDDLE

I'M IN THE DARK.

I've come to the point of wondering if there are special places where miracles might happen. After all, you never know. Would they be hard to reach though, or just a little bit further on from here? If I ran, could I get there? It's not clear where such ideas come from, they just seem to crop up out of nowhere. That's fairly miraculous in itself, it seems to me. Just one of life's fantasies, I know, though I'm thinking of running all the same. Right now that's impossible, of course. In all honesty, how could I? You have to walk before you can run, and before that you have to stand on your own two feet. Part of me can't bear the thought. Yes, I'm coiled in the dark, starting from the O of nothing, I know that. Call it the darkness before time — before *my* time. These are the thoughts which come to me while I'm hidden away, the dreams I have in the sack.

The darkness can do funny things to your way of seeing. And it's all dark silence here, so much so it almost feels as if I don't exist. But I do really, and when the moment's right, I'll come out. I'll burst out of here with a great cry. The end's in sight now, even though part of me doesn't wish to reach it. Being here could be the thing I'm best at, who knows what the future has in store? I live with all the dark possibilities and all the light hopes. I'm everywhere and nowhere at all.

But I don't have so long to go, I can already feel the pull of the world. Sometimes I even hear the world's voices. A rattle and a shake, a faint *brrrrrr*, and a *zzzzzzzz*. Somewhere. I'll be out of here when the time comes, but you can't rush such things, it takes as long as it takes. Asking why is a faded question, I let it go a while back.

I'm already less fluid and undecided than I was a moment ago and I sense life slip in closer and take possession. With every passing minute I feel a little more defined. Fear darts in suddenly, and makes me want to

CLOUDING THE LIGHT

stay where I am forever. The light out there's too bright for comfort and my instinct's telling me I need to keep right away from it. So though I can sense them trying to get me out, I'm resisting it as hard as I can. They won't let me alone though, will they. There's a slap-slapping, they want to prise me out of my hiding place. They all know I'm in here, I can't be seen, but all the same I'm not invisible. The huge body-sized sack is on show to anybody who cares to look and it's clear they want me out. Not that they can help it, the expectations have been set up this way. They want me to provide a miracle. I roll one way, then the other. I'm already working my hands to make it happen. Soon.

I'M ALL IN GREEN.

Either I'm waiting to emerge from this chrysalis or I'm finished. In the centre, here, I'm not quite sure which it's to be. When I swing forward through the boughs, I could be diving or soaring. Or if the movement's only imaginary, I could be waiting for the right conditions to atrophy in my sack. I'd say a lot of things in life must be taken in different ways like this. I try concentrating, to see if I can find the answer within myself, but it's no use, I can only talk about the green in the here and now. The lush green foliage. I'm part of it, or I'm breaking through it or I'm falling. We don't know where we're going till we're there. I do know one thing—it's dangerous to stray too far from the colour of the moment. Not that you're safe in green. Fresh dangers here before you even move. Around me the trees, the wider wood. May green. Sap. Leap. The sap leaps in the green May. Bulge-belly geniality. Acorns are sprouting. Some will become oak trees, most won't make it. Will I, in my crown of leaves, be one of those? Maybe you always *do* know what your destiny's going to be, even if you avoid looking; you sense the words imprinted across your cheeks. Even though you mightn't know where they came from. There again, at another level I don't believe anything I'm told. I laugh lustily and find it's a great release doing that. *Itum Titum Paraditum.*

I open my mouth and sap spurts out.

GOD OF THE PIGEONS

I'M INTO THIEVING.

One of the few things that doesn't dismay me. I know where I am in the taking-moment. I take what's mine and what's not in equal measures, not choosing to make the distinction. I'm expedient, a twirling pragmatist. I steal anything and everything small enough to get into my special pocket, I have dexterous hands. I could be floating up to the top of the sky, I could be sinking. Frequently I don't know where I am, but stealing is what grounds me. *Abracadabra!*

If you're caught thieving you can expect punishment. What I say is, think of the planet, think of fundamental nature, just there, unowned. But there are these little marked off bits of space everywhere you look, territories set out with pegs and wire by people who describe themselves as the owners. They wave their flags, looking bloody ridiculous, they've set up rules of ownership which you have to go along with. If not, *xxxxx*.

And here, I'm making the throat-slitting gesture, meaning you're finished. Except it's always a bit of a joke, isn't it. Nobody's going to shed any tears if they see someone running their forefinger along their upheld throat, and making the face that goes with this, and making the *xxxxx* noise. Will they.

Which is the way it should be.

Anyway, you can't see my hands. And supposing I really am just taking what's mine. Me and mine, meany miney. My body occupying space within this sack. No one can see me but everybody knows where I am. Swinging here from left to right is easy. I feel preoccupied, slightly dazed. It's a seductive motion, swinging like a pendulum. It's good being here like this; a steal. Meaning a bargain of some kind, meaning it's all free.

I CANNOT EAT THE FOOD I SEE.

Luscious fruits hang from the trees around me. The ultimate temptation to the starving man. When I lean forward to reach them they recede or vanish altogether. The art of the impossible. I've learned its ways by now. It seeps through me. I'd like to be happy but I can't stop crying out

RIDDLE

for water. For all the water everywhere which I'll never ever get to taste. Just to let it moisten my lips would be great, but I've learned the hard way it won't be possible for me to quite reach it. Every time I lean forward I feel the excitement though, as if this time... *this time*... then it's back to square one. If that's the place where agony starts.

A rock's overhanging me. My head is always in its shadow, so I'll never be able to forget this. If time moves the picture will change immediately. The rock will fall, I'll be finished. And I'm condemned to imagining time moving and me being crushed, living through the tragedy a million times over. Before my eyes are the figs, the peaches, the apples and the dates and whatever other fruits can be thought.

But you know I'm kidding, don't you. What's my name?

I'm the story you want to happen. I'm some primaeval desire you have, nothing in myself. I create victims for you, killing and eating flesh. When I blab the secrets of the *haves* to the *have-nots*, I'm committing sin big-time for you; when I squander the Ambrosia of your gods and laugh.

In the dark it's easy to imagine I don't exist. But I'm getting out of here. Soon. My hands are already unclicking the little catches, they're at the underside of the ropes now, loosening. You'll see what you want to see. A miracle which comes popping up out of nowhere, or a trick. Either way, it's not a thing you'll come across every day, either way, seeing is believing. A trick question and answer. You'll laugh your head off at my cheating game.

I CAN PICTURE THE SKY.

One of me can — one of *us*. It's singularly hard to reach. One of my arms stretches towards a bright slit of it. No colour visible as yet, this is before colour, don't forget, before most things. But light is there and suddenly, somehow, I need it. Well, part of me does. One of my eyes drinks it in, my other eye closes its lid. So there you have me. Put both my halves together and you have the folly of two about to happen.

Well, the end of darkness is in sight. I'll make your dreams come true Begin your clapping and rhythmical chanting, say the word, let me hear the music of your need, as I work myself upwards to the slit of sky. One of my eyes is loving what it sees, the other won't look anywhere but inwards. Pain and pleasure of all this contradiction. But the light's there, out of the blue, to confirm what you've wanted to hear, that there's more than one of me doing the terrible things I do. You'll be happy, I know, because that above everything is what you want me for. To break as many social rules and natural laws as I come across, and resist any attempt to be whittled down into one unified personality. You love my defiance and my diversity. If I can do it nobody else needs to. Who made me? You made me. I see the sky for all of us, you needn't bother to look. I'm putting my finger through the gap, next I'm putting my hand through. Tugging and tearing on the primaeval cord. I lean up, biting the end of it through with my teeth. *Snip.* I don't just imagine the sound of clapping, I really hear it. Some of the perspicacious ones have already seen the long side of my thumb, maybe a quick fuzzy darting of my lower arm. Yes, they know I'm here in a more thorough way now. Not that they ever doubted it completely. I must make a sign of recognition. Take my bow before they finish me off.

I AM REBORN.

You can't say *born*, as such, because everyone present saw me being wrapped up in here, saw my hands locked behind me in metal cuffs, saw the key put somewhere I couldn't hope to reach. Not only that, but they know it's not my first time around. I've been brought back before and it's a fair bet this is a repeat performance. They saw me go in the sack, they saw the sack go in the trunk, saw the trunk locked and bolted. So, no getting away from it. I was bound up like a chrysalis, yet everybody trusted me to know the ropes. Ha.

Yes, I can tell you I was out of that same trunk in three minutes flat and lying on the hard ground, my sack bulging, me squirming inside it. Got to make a bit of a show—the struggle of life about to force itself into the open. A living drama. As the silences and shouts of the crowd reach through to me. The floor is stone, I roll and writhe. I'm in the dark, then

RIDDLE

all at once I start to see. I can be seen. I fling up my hands, the handcuffs fly out. The sack falls away from me. I'm in the portico of a church, the crowd curves round me like a bay. Lapping. I can feel the ripples. A semicircle of clapping hands. Here we are in Covent Garden, I look up and see cheering drinkers on the balconies of wine bars lifting their glasses down to me. All in bright light. I, who in the shade cast by the pillars of this church am a bit obscure, as always. It's the Actors' Church. St Paul's, Covent Garden, Inigo Jones, 1624. So here I am, stepping out of the rough old sack that I've been rolling around in for a good five minutes or more. It's a miracle I'm still in one piece. I've been everywhere and nowhere for you, a funny kind of journey. By my TRICKS you shall know me, if you're to know me at all. I don't mean what I say and I don't say what I mean.

WHAT AM I?

ACKNOWLEDGEMENTS

The author would like to thank the editors of the following publications where stories from this collection first published, either in full or as an extract:

'Clouding the Light' in *The London Miscellany*, 2010; 'Beauty Queens' in *Trespass*, 2009; 'Entertaining Angie' in *Brand*, 2009; 'Riddle' in *Orbis*, 2009; 'Making Dracula' in *Chroma*, 2007; 'Mimosa, House of Dream' in *Prophecy*, 2007; 'Squeeze' in *Texts Bones*, 2006; 'Batman' in *BuzzWords*, 2004; 'Little Elva' in *Dream Catcher*, 2004; 'Racetrack' in *Tears in the Fence*, 2004 'Can I Be Dandini?' in *Tears in the Fence*, 2002.